"And now you're telling me you haven't got one room available in this entire hotel?"

"I'm afraid that is correct, sir. Well, we do have an accommodation, but—"

"We'll take it."

Dana touched Griffin's arm. "McKenna," she whispered.

Griffin swung towards her. "What?"

She looked at the clerk, then at him. "We cannot share a room."

"Did you hear what the man said? This room he's offering us is all there is."

"I don't care. There is no way I am going to share a room with—"

"Oh, it isn't a room, madam."

Griffin and Dana both looked at the clerk, who swallowed nervously.

"It's a suite."

A slow smile edged across Griffin's face. "A suite? Don't tell me. What is it? The Presidential Suite?"

The clerk looked from Griffin to Dana. She could almost feel his distress. "Not exactly, sir," he said, and cleared his throat. "It's—it's the Bridal Suite."

Anything can happen behind closed doors!

Do you dare find out...?

Some of your favorite Harlequin Presents® authors
are exploring this delicious fantasy in our sizzling,
sensual miniseries DO NOT DISTURB!

Circumstances throw different couples together in a
whirlwind of unexpected attraction. Forced into each
other's company whether they like it or not, they're
soon in the grip of passion—and definitely *don't*
want to be disturbed!

Coming next month:

Honeymoon Baby
by
Susan Napier
Harlequin Presents #1985

SANDRA MARTON

The Bridal Suite

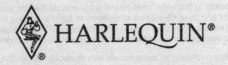

TORONTO • NEW YORK • LONDON
AMSTERDAM • PARIS • SYDNEY • HAMBURG
STOCKHOLM • ATHENS • TOKYO • MILAN • MADRID
PRAGUE • WARSAW • BUDAPEST • AUCKLAND

ISBN 0-373-11979-8

THE BRIDAL SUITE

First North American Publication 1998.

CHAPTER ONE

GRIFFIN MCKENNA was a pirate.

The newspapers, and the Wall Street pundits, said he was a financial genius, but Dana Anderson knew better. McKenna was a pirate, plain and simple. He took whatever he wanted, whether it was a corporation or a woman.

What else could you call a man like that?

Gorgeous, that was what, according to the gossip columns. Dana supposed there were some women who'd find him attractive. The sapphire-blue eyes, the thick, silky black hair, the cleft chin and the nose that was almost perfectly straight except for a faint bend in the middle...all of it seemed exactly right for McKenna's broad-shouldered, long-legged body.

So what? Nobody'd ever said pirates had to be homely.

McKenna bought companies that were in trouble, scooping them up like a kid taking candy from a dish, and turned them into moneymakers. And, they said, he managed such feats because he had skill, courage and determination. They left out the fact that he'd also started life with an inheritance big enough to float a small kingdom, or that he got obvious pleasure from controlling the destinies of others.

And from having people fawn over him—especially women.

But not all women, thought Dana as she marched down the hall to McKenna's office. No, definitely not all. She, for instance, was not the least bit impressed by the man. She'd seen him, early on, for what he was. Not just a pirate but a charter member of the Good Old Boys club. An arrogant, egotistical, self-important Male Chauvinist, capital M, capital C.

What he needed, instead of gushing columnists and swooning females, was the truth.

Well, she was about to deliver it.

She paused outside his office.

Not the truth about his overrated, overpublicized self. Dana wasn't a fool. She had more than a job here, at Data Bytes; she had a career, one she'd worked damn hard for, and she intended to keep it. The truth she'd tell him, the truth he needed to learn, was about the company's all-new, highly touted computer program, the one that was going to be on display at the big software convention in Miami this coming weekend—the program that was supposed to save Data Bytes from going belly-up.

But it wouldn't. It couldn't, because the code that underlay it was a disaster.

She'd already tried telling that to McKenna a week ago.

"Mr. McKenna is a very busy man," his secretary, the formidable Miss Macy, had said. Dana had replied that The Very Busy Man himself had made it clear, during the organizational meeting he'd held, that he was also A Very Approachable Man.

She hadn't mentioned that he'd also made it clear he was a man who believed in gender equality the way a skunk believed in deodorants.

Not that it came as a surprise. What kind of man got his name into the gossip columns all the time? What kind of man was photographed with a different woman each week?

What kind of man made the sort of joke McKenna had made at that organizational meeting?

"Remember," he'd intoned solemnly, "we're all in this together, people. If Data Bytes is going to fulfill the vision I have for it—and I assure you, it will—it'll be because every man here works his tail off to make it happen."

"Every man, and woman," Jeannie Aarons had called out, and McKenna had grinned along with all the others.

"An interesting observation," he'd said with wide-eyed innocence, and, after the laughter had died down, he'd added that he never doubted the value of the "female of the species."

"I'll just bet you don't," Dana had muttered under her breath.

If she had any lingering doubts, McKenna had swept them aside when she'd met with him last week, after Macy had finally agreed to grant her an audience. She had come armed with printouts to support her contention that the new code was not going to be ready on time—but McKenna hadn't been the least bit interested in listening.

"How do you do?" he'd said, rising from behind his desk like an emperor greeting his subject. "Would you care for some coffee? Some tea?"

"Nothing, thank you," Dana had said politely, and then she'd launched into her speech only to have McKenna cut her off in the middle with an imperious wave of the hand.

"Yes, yes," he'd said. "Dave told me that he thought you might come by to protest."

"I'm not protesting, sir," Dana started to say, but then his words hit home. "Dave *told* you? You mean, you already know there's a problem?" It was such a relief, knowing Dave had finally faced reality, that she smiled. "Well, I'm glad to hear it. I never dreamed—"

"—That you'd be passed over for promotion." McKenna nodded. "Dave explained that to me. He understands why that's made you unhappy."

"I *was* passed over. But that isn't why—"

"He also told me that you've complained that you haven't been given enough credit for your work."

"Complained?"

"Politely, of course." McKenna flashed a patronizing smile. "He assured me you were every inch the lady when you brought it to his attention."

"Did he," Dana said coolly.

"He was very open," McKenna said. He smiled again, this time with unctuous sympathy. "You see, we go back a long way together, Dave and I. We belonged to the same fraternity."

"Do tell," Dana said, even more coldly.

"I assure you, Miss Anderson, your efforts will not go unrewarded. I'm going to institute a bonus plan, and—"

"Mr. McKenna," Dana took a steadying breath. "This isn't about getting credit for my work, or about that promotion. I came to tell you that the new code isn't going to work! If you introduce it at the Miami conference—"

"Not 'if,' Miss Anderson. When. And it won't be me introducing it, it will be Dave. I suppose you'd hoped for that chance yourself, but—"

"Oh, for heaven's sake!" Dana shot to her feet and glared at him. "I'm not looking for a shoulder to weep on, dammit! I came to warn you that the code's a mess, but if you don't want to hear it, there's nothing I can do."

"And why is it a mess, Miss Anderson?"

"Because..." Dana hesitated. Because Dave's a drunk, she'd almost said, but McKenna would never believe her. "Because it's got bugs. Little bits of code that are written wrong."

"So Dave tells me. He also tells me you wrote those little bits of code, Miss Anderson. Not that he or I hold you responsible, of course, considering your lack of experience."

"My what?"

"But he assured me that you'll learn. He says you're bright, and quick."

Dana stared at him in astonishment. "I don't believe this. I absolutely don't—"

"And now, if you'll forgive me..." McKenna had smiled politely as he rose to his feet, came around his desk and lightly grasped her elbow. "Thank you for stopping by," he'd said in a way that made it clear she was dismissed. "My door is always open to my employees, Miss Anderson—or may I call you Dana?"

Dana, who'd been so angry by then that she could hardly see straight, had pulled free of his grasp.

"You may call me *Ms.* Anderson," she'd snapped.

And what a stupid thing that had been to say. Even now, the memory made her shudder. Nobody, *nobody,* at Data Bytes was so ridiculously formal. People went around in jeans and T-shirts with funny sayings on them. Why, she was the only one who dressed in suits and tailored shirts, but when you sat down to pee instead of standing up, you had to work harder at winning a place on the team. Despite all the gender equality laws, the playing field was far from equal. Just look at how McKenna had thought he was complimenting her last week, telling her she was a lady....

"Miss Anderson. Sorry. I meant, *Ms.* Anderson, of course."

The familiar voice, a sort of honeyed growl, came from just behind her. Dana swung around and found herself facing Griffin McKenna.

"Mr. McKenna. I didn't—I thought—"

"Tongue-tied, Ms. Anderson? How very unusual."

Dana blushed. How could he manage that? He had a way of making her feel—what was the word? Incompetent? No. Not that. She knew her stuff; you didn't get as far as she'd gotten on the corporate ladder without being damn good at what you did. Uncertain. Yes, that was it. He made her feel uncertain. It had to do with that little smile on his mouth when he looked at her, as if he knew something she didn't.

"Were you looking for me? Or were you simply planning on skulking in the hallway?"

"I have never skulked in my life, Mr. McKenna. Yes, as a matter of fact, I was looking for you. We need to talk."

McKenna's brows lifted. "Again?"

"Again," she said, holding her ground.

"Well..." He shot back his cuff, frowned at his watch, then nodded. "I suppose I can give you a few minutes."

Such generosity! Dana forced a smile to her lips.

"Thank you," she said, and strode through the door ahead of him, past a surprised-looking Miss Macy, who was guarding McKenna's lair with her usual dragon-like efficiency, and into his office.

"She doesn't have an appointment, sir," the Dragon hissed.

"That's all right, Miss Macy," McKenna said soothingly. He paused, just long enough to give the Anderson babe time to stalk halfway across the carpet toward his desk. It was the polite thing to do, but hell, who was he kidding? What he wanted was the view.

And there it was.

Ms. Anderson had the walk of a lioness, all power and pride, and the golden hair to match. And her eyes, when she turned to face him...they were the color of emeralds. Her mouth was lush and soft-looking, made all the more tempting because she never seemed to bother with lipstick. And oh, that body, curved and feminine despite the dowdy suits she wore....

Griffin closed the door and leaned back against it, arms folded over his chest.

It certainly was a pity that a woman who looked like this should be such a cold piece of work. But then, Dave had warned him.

"The Anderson babe's a hard case, Griff," he'd said. "You know the type. She wishes to God she'd been born a guy but since she wasn't, she holds every man since Adam responsible for the world's woes."

Griffin sighed, walked to his desk and sat down behind it. Why did some women want to be what Nature had not meant them to be? He'd never been able to understand it.

"Well, Ms. Anderson," he said, "what can I do for you today?"

Dana cleared her throat. "Mr. McKenna—"

What was he doing? Dana frowned. He was looking through the stack of papers on his desk, *that's* what he was doing.

"Mr. McKenna?"

He looked up. "Hmm?"

"Sir, I was trying to tell you about—"

He was doing it again! Bending that dark head of his, thumbing through what appeared to be a bunch of telephone memos, instead of paying attention to her.

"Mr. McKenna. I'd appreciate it if you'd listen."

"Sorry."

He looked up, and she could tell from the expression on his face that he wasn't the least bit sorry. As far as he was concerned, she was wasting his time.

Dana took a deep breath.

"I ran the new program this morning," she said.

"And?"

"And, it's a total disaster. There's no way it'll perform properly tomorrow, when you demo it at the Miami convention."

McKenna favored her with a small smile. "Fortunately for me, I won't be doing the demo, remember? Dave will."

Stupid, stupid man! Dana smiled politely in return.

"It won't matter who does it," she said calmly. "The point I'm trying to make is that the code won't work right. And Dave won't—"

"It's really a pity, you know."

"What's a pity?"

"That you should be so distressed by that missed promotion."

"That I should be...? Mr. McKenna, I told you, this has absolutely nothing to do with—"

"Your record is excellent, Miss—sorry—*Ms.* Anderson," McKenna leaned forward over his desk, his eyes focused on hers, his expression one of heartfelt compassion. "I took the time to look through it, after our chat last week."

Lord, he was condescending! Dana's gaze narrowed.

"Thank you, but I don't need reassurance. I'm good at what I do. Very good. I know that. I spent a lot of time on that code, a *lot* of time, but Dave—"

McKenna got to his feet.

"I'd hate to see this become an obsession, Ms. Anderson," His voice was polite, but his smile, this time, was cool. "You're a valued employee, but so is Forrester. And he's the man in charge."

"Exactly," Dana said before she could stop herself. "He's the *man* in charge."

"He is the right *person* for the job, Ms. Anderson. His gender has nothing to do with it. As for you... I suggest you rethink your position. Data Bytes would like to keep you—

but if you're not happy being part of the team, perhaps you might wish to move on.''

Dana had always prided herself on being a clear-thinking woman. She knew it was one of her best attributes, that cool, rational approach to life. It was why she'd succeeded at virtually everything she'd attempted, from the A's she'd collected in elementary school straight through to the Phi Beta Kappa key she'd proudly acquired at Harvard.

And yet, at that moment, she wanted nothing more than to tell Griffin McKenna what he could do with his advice and his job.

But she couldn't. She wouldn't. Her life, and her career, were moving forward just as she'd planned, or they had been, until the despicable McKenna came along. And she'd be damned if she'd let him derail all her plans.

"Ms. Anderson? Do I make myself clear?"

Dana forced herself to meet his cold glare with equanimity.

"Perfectly," she said calmly. "Good afternoon, Mr. McKenna.''

And she turned on her heel and marched out of his office without a backward glance.

Dana banged open the door to the ladies' room.

McKenna wasn't despicable, he was detestable.

"The bastard," she said between her teeth. She stalked to the nearest white porcelain sink, turned on the faucet, cupped her hands under the flow and splashed cold water over her burning cheeks. "The thick-skulled, insensitive lout!"

She yanked a paper towel from the dispenser, scrubbed it over her face, then balled it up and dumped it into the waste receptacle.

Was he blind? He'd bought his success with inherited money, but he did have some degree of talent. Everybody said so. Even Arthur, who knew about such things, said so.

"My dear," he'd informed her after McKenna's takeover, "the man is a financial genius.''

Dana had been so ticked off at hearing Arthur, of all people, say such a thing that the "my dear" had slid past her, instead of making her clench her teeth as it usually did.

"Financial genius, my foot," she'd replied. "He's a spoiled brat, born with an 18-karat spoon in his mouth."

Arthur had set her straight, explaining that McKenna had been born to money, yes, but that even the most conservative analysts figured he'd tripled his inherited wealth by now.

"If you'd read the *Journal*," Arthur had said kindly, "you'd be aware that the man knows all there is to know about leveraging stocks and corporate takeovers."

Well, maybe he did. Dana leaned back against the sink, arms folded, and glared at the row of closed stalls. But he didn't know spit about computers, or computer programs, and it was painfully obvious that he didn't know spit about her boss, either. Dave was running their department into the ground, but when she'd tried to tell that to McKenna, he'd damn near laughed in her face. And why?

Because he and Forrester were pals, that was why. Because she could never qualify as anybody's "pal," not so long as she was a woman, and never mind McKenna's remark about gender having nothing to do with it. Dana might have come out of college naive enough to believe that sexism in the office—especially in the programming field—was a whisper of the past, but five years in the trenches had taught her otherwise.

If you were a man, the sky was the limit. But if you were a woman, there was a glass ceiling. And she had reached it.

The only kind of female the McKennas of this world could deal with were the ones who knew how to flutter their lashes. McKenna, especially. If he hadn't been linked with every beautiful female on the planet, it was only because, at thirty-five, he hadn't yet had the time to get around to them all.

One Down, a tabloid headline had read the day after John Kennedy Jr. tied the knot. One to Go.

Even Arthur had understood just who that "one" was.

Dana stamped her foot. If she'd swooned at his feet, he'd have paid attention to her. If she'd been a man, bringing him bad news about the new code, he'd have listened. But she hadn't swooned, and she wasn't male, and so he'd shooed her off as if she were a bothersome fly.

"The idiot!" Dana said, swinging toward the mirror.

The door swung open and Jeannie Aarons walked into the room.

"Don't even speak to me," Dana said crossly.

Jeannie's brows arched. "And a bright and cheery hello to you, too."

"How does that man live with himself? He is, without question, the most thick-skulled, miserable son of a—"

"Arthur? Thick-skulled, yes. Dull, yes. But miserable's going too far," Jeannie leaned closer to the mirror, eyes narrowed, and peered at her chin. "Wonderful. I'm getting a zit, and tonight I'm seeing that guy I met at that singles dance. What do you think, huh? Should I try popping it?"

"I'm not talking about Arthur. I'm talking about McKenna. Who does the man think he is? Who in *hell* does he think he is?"

"A hunk. That's who."

"A jerk. *That's* who. The smug, miserable, rotten—"

"My grandma always said that repetition was the product of a non-creative mind."

"Your grandma never met Mr. I-Am-God McKenna. Jeannie, what *are* you doing?"

"Squeezing this zit. I cannot possibly go out tonight with a zit the size of Rhode Island on my chin. It's gross."

Dana sighed. "No, it isn't."

"Yes, it is. I look like the poster child for leprosy."

"Do you have any concealer with you?"

"Does an elephant have a trunk?"

"Well, give it to me. And your compact. I'll fix it so your zit will disappear. I just wish somebody could do the same to His Majesty McKenna."

"Now, Dana." Obediently, Jeannie let her face be tilted up toward the light. "Wanting to fix McKenna isn't nice."

"Why not? Fixing that man's butt would be doing the world a favor."

Jeannie grinned. "Ah. Well, fixing his *butt* is okay, I guess, but fixing *him,* as in the way a vet fixes a randy tomcat, would make legions of damsels weep."

"Frankly," Dana said coldly, "I don't give a hoot about his personal life, though the way he goes through women, he might just deserve it."

"I take it you're not one of his fans," Jeannie said cheerfully.

"If you mean that I'm not taken in by his press, his money or his looks, you're right."

"There's no sense in arguing over his looks. Only a troglodyte wouldn't find the guy hunky. As for his press... according to what I've heard, Griffin McKenna bought up and turned around a lot of troubled companies last year."

"Great. First Arthur and now you, giving me the same speech."

"Please! Don't put me in the same sentence with Arthur. I'm liable to fall asleep from boredom."

"It's garbage and you know it," Dana said, ignoring the gibe. "McKenna is a pirate."

"Does he still insist on wearing bow ties?"

"McKenna?" Dana said, staring at Jeannie.

"Arthur. Somebody ought to tell him, guys just don't wear those things anymore."

"I think his bow ties make him look distinguished," Dana said loyally. "Besides, I was talking about McKenna, and please don't bother telling me how many jobs he's saved because that's all secondary to his real purpose in life, which is to make himself as disgustingly rich as possible."

"My, oh, my, is that right? He should be taken out and shot."

"And to accumulate as many female scalps as he can manage in his spare time. Turn toward me a little, please."

"I thought you just said you don't care about his personal life."

"I don't. It's just that his attitude toward women spills over into his work."

"Whoa." Jeannie drew in her breath. "Don't tell me," she said in an excited whisper. "He made a pass?"

"Ha!"

"Ha, as in yes?"

"Ha, as in I almost wish he had." Dana's eyes glittered. "Then, at least, I could nail him with the charges he deserves. The man is a sexist pig. He sees women only as objects."

"I thought you said he didn't make a pass," Jeannie said in bewilderment.

"He didn't," Dana stepped back, cocked her head and studied Jeannie's face. "There. If you keep your hands away from your chin, nobody'll notice a thing."

Jeannie swung toward the mirror. "Terrific! I'm almost human again."

"Which is more than we can say of Mister McKenna." Dana curved her hands around the rim of the sink and glared into the mirror. "Tell me the truth, please. Do I sound like an idiot?"

Jeannie looked at her friend and sighed. "Your trouble isn't what you sound like, my friend. It's what you look like. People who design complicated computer programs aren't supposed to look like Michelle Pfeiffer stand-ins. Well, except for the hair. If you'd just go blonder, leave it loose..."

"Forget about the way I look," Dana said sharply, "although that, clearly, is part of the problem as far as McKenna's concerned. He looks at me, all he can see is a female."

"How peculiar," Jeannie said sweetly.

"Sitting there, like an emperor on his throne, giving me these solemn looks, nodding wisely as if he were really listening to what I was saying, when he'd already decided I had nothing worth listening to, thanks to my chromosomes. Oh, it was as plain as the nose on your face."

"Or the Mount Vesuvius on my chin," Jeannie swung toward the mirror and frowned. "When did this happen? When did McKenna decide you had terminal PMS?"

"Last week. Well, and again just a few minutes ago. I met with him twice, and each time was a disaster." Dana paced across the room. "He didn't listen to me, Jeannie, he patronized me. And when that didn't work, he told me that I could look for another job, if I didn't like this one."

"Uh-oh. That sounds ominous."

"And why?"

"Well," Jeannie said, "I guess because—"

"Because I stood up to him, that's why. Because I turned out not to be the ladylike little puppet he thought I was, one that would let him pull my strings."

"I don't think puppets have strings," Jeannie said carefully. "I mean, it's marionettes that—"

"It was just a figure of speech," Dana said angrily. "Oh, that man. How can he be so blind?"

"Dana, look, I think maybe you're going overboard, you know?"

"Well, you think wrong. There's a serious problem with the new code, thanks to my boss. Dave's screwing up, big time."

"Are you sure?"

"I'm positive," Dana took a deep breath. "He's got a drinking problem."

"You're joking."

"I'm dead serious. He doesn't slur his speech or fall down in a heap, but there are times he's so drunk he can hardly see the monitor."

"But—but surely, someone would have noticed—"

"Someone did. Me."

"Did you say something about it to him?"

"Yes, of course."

"And?"

"And, he denied it. Then he said that no one would believe me. He's the one with a name. With experience. So now I spend half my time trying to catch his errors, and the other half trying to keep up with my own work, and the result is that everything's a total mess."

Jeannie chewed on her lip. "Damn," she said softly. "What

a spot to be in. Well, you'll just have to go to McKenna. I know snitching on Dave won't be fun, but—''

"I *have* gone to him," Dana said furiously. "What do you think I've been telling you for the last fifteen minutes?"

"You told him Dave's a drunk?"

"No. I knew he'd never believe me. But I told him the code's unstable."

"What did he say?"

"He said he knows there are problems, and that Dave told him I was the cause, and that he realizes I'm upset because I didn't get that promotion." Dana's eyes flashed. "And, until he got around to telling me I might want to look for another job, he complimented me for complaining in such a ladylike way—''

The door swung open. Charlie, the custodian, beamed at Dana and Jeannie. He had a mop in one hand and a bucket in the other.

"Top o' the mornin', ladies," he said cheerfully. "My apologies for disturbin' you. I did knock, but I guess you didn't hear me."

"That's okay," Jeannie shot a glance at Dana. "We were just about finished in here."

"Makin' girl talk, were you?" Charlie beamed his grandfatherly smile. "And primpin', I suppose. Well, darlins! you can rest assured that there's no need. The both of you ladies are perfect, just as you are."

Jeannie smothered a groan as she saw the look on Dana's face.

"Indeed," Dana said coldly. "Whatever would we *girls* do without a man's stamp of approval?"

Charlie, blissfully unaware of the quicksand beneath his feet, grinned broadly. "Isn't that a fact?"

"You want a fact?" Dana demanded, marching toward him. Charlie's smile faded and he flattened himself against the wall. "We are not girls," she said, wagging her finger under his nose, "and we are not ladies. We are women. As for needing a man's stamp of approval—''

Jeannie grabbed Dana's arm and hustled her from the bathroom. Halfway out the door, she turned and gave Charlie an apologetic smile. "It's nothing personal," she hissed. "She's just upset."

"I am not upset," Dana said, spinning around. "I am just tired of pretending that I need patting on the head, as if I were a—a poodle instead of a person."

Charlie's baffled glance went from one woman to the other. "I never said one word against poodles, Miss."

"Oh, for heaven's sake! I didn't... This has nothing to do with dogs. I simply meant..." Dana threw up her arms. "Men," she snorted, and marched off.

Moments later, Charlie stood before Griffin McKenna's massive desk, his bushy white brows still drawn together in a knot.

"So, there I was, about to mop the ladies' room—pardon me, the women's room—and the next thing I knew, the young lady said I'd insulted her dog. I ask you, sir, why would I? I like dogs. 'Course, she says it's a poodle. Try as I might, I can't claim to be fond of them little things. Can't stand their yappin' all the time, if you know what I mean."

Griffin nodded wisely. That was the way he hoped it looked, at any rate, but he couldn't be sure he was pulling it off. What in hell was the old guy babbling about?

He liked Charlie. But his mind was on other things. Like putting on a good showing at the convention that started tomorrow in Miami. Like landing a couple of big accounts with Data Bytes's new financial database program, to put the company back in the black.

Like figuring out why a woman as gorgeous as Dana Anderson should be so impossible.

Griffin frowned. Why waste time thinking about her? She was gorgeous, yeah, but she was nothing but a pain in the rear. If only she'd admit she didn't know everything, and do what she was told.

Not that he could imagine that happening. The perfect Ms. Anderson taking orders? And from a man? He almost laughed.

Still, there had to be some guy out there, somewhere, who could tame her. It wouldn't be easy, but it would be worth it to turn all that anger and fire and single-minded determination into passion, the sort of passion beautiful women were meant to experience.

"...Just said that the two of 'em were pretty little things. I suppose her poodle is, too."

Griffin dragged his thoughts back to Charlie. The poor guy was really worked up, but about what? Griffin was no closer to an answer now than he'd been when the old fellow first came bustling through the door five minutes ago, with the ferocious Miss Macy snapping at his heels. The woman was a leftover from prior management and insisted on defending the door to his office with the zeal of a junkyard dog, despite all his reminders that Data Bytes's employees were free to see him, anytime, anyplace, about anything.

"...Wife's sister had a poodle once. Nasty little thing it was, all teeth and a bark high enough to make your ears ring."

Griffin nodded in sympathy. He leaned forward, picked up his pen and scribbled a note on the pad Macy had centered neatly on his desk blotter.

"Early retirement package for Macy?" he wrote. "Put junk-yard dog out to pasture." Which was a mixed metaphor if ever he'd seen one. It was just that Charlie kept going on about dogs...

Griffin focused his attention on the old man who surely deserved it, considering that he'd made it past Macy, and with his mop and scrub bucket still in his hands.

"...Best come straight to you, sir, seein' as you said there was an open door policy. Right?"

"Right. Absolutely." Griffin cleared his throat. "Although, actually, I'm not quite certain what the problem seems to—"

"Well, sir, the young lady thinks I insulted her and maybe even her poodle. And I didn't."

Griffin rubbed his hand across his forehead. This was what came of defying your own advisors, all of whom thought he was crazy to go in and spend a couple of months at the helm of each company he purchased. He'd always disagreed...until now.

"Who knows what she'll do? Complain to you, I s'pose. All this nonsense I read, about sexual harrass...whatever." Charlie looked stricken. "She had this real angry look in her eyes—green, they are, and cold as can be."

An icy draft seemed to waft across the back of Griffin's neck. "She has green eyes?"

"Yes, sir. It had been on the tip of my tongue to tell her they were the color of emeralds but, thank the saints, I never got that far. Anyways, I thought I might do well to come and talk with you."

"And the lady's name?" Griffin asked, though he knew. Dammit, he knew.

"Her friend called her—did I mention there were two young ladies, Mr. McKenna?"

"Yes. Yes, you did. What did her friend call her, Charlie?"

"Dana. And if I never see the woman again, it'll be way too soon. You understand, sir?"

Did he understand? Griffin smiled tightly as he rose to his feet and offered Charlie his hand.

"I hope I did the right thing, comin' to you, sir," Charlie said. "I don't want to get the girl—the woman—in any trouble, you understand."

"Wipe her from your mind, Charlie. You won't have any more problems with Dana Anderson."

"You'll have a talk with her, will you? Tell her I didn't mean to insult her dog?"

"Indeed," Griffin said as he eased the old man out the door and shut it after him.

Oh, yes. He'd have a talk with Ms. Dana Anderson. Damn right, he would. The woman was trying to make Dave look bad, and now she'd upset a nice old man. She was Trouble with a capital T, and eliminating trouble was what Griffin did best.

Whistling softly between his teeth, he strolled to his desk. His glance fell on the note he'd made about Macy. With a sigh, he grabbed it, crumpled it up and slam-dunked it into the wastepaper basket.

Macy was a dragon, but she was a dragon who knew how to do her job.

Dana Anderson was a different story. Let her go make life difficult for somebody else. Let her bake cakes, or sew curtains, take dictation or type letters, let her do a woman's job instead of storming into the business world and making trouble. And if she couldn't accept her rightful place in life, then she could go find a bunch of leftover female twit-heads from the seventies, rip off her bra and burn it.

Griffin caught his breath. An image filled his mind. He saw Dana standing beside a blazing fire, her green eyes locked to his as she let down that mass of streaked golden hair and then, with heart-stopping slowness, took off not just her bra but every stitch she wore, until she had nothing on except her own soft, rose-flushed skin.

Naked, she'd be even lovelier than he'd dreamed. And yes, dammit, he *had* dreamed of her, though it galled him to admit it.

Griffin shut his eyes. The image was so real. He could feel the heat of the fire and hear the soft beat of drums somewhere off in the darkness of the night. He could see Dana smile, then run the tip of her tongue across her lips. Her hands lifted; she thrust them into her hair. Her head fell back and she began to dance. For him. Only for him...

Griffin blinked, cursed, and grabbed for the telephone.

"Miss Macy," he barked. "Send Dana Anderson in here, on the double."

"Mr. Forrester's here. He wants to see you, sir."

"All right, send him in. And then get hold of the Anderson woman."

"Of course, sir."

Griffin sat down. He'd give Forrester five minutes, although, to tell the truth, the man was becoming an annoyance. Still, there was no harm in a little delay. In fact, it would make what came next all the sweeter, when he finally gave the blonde with the green eyes and the disposition of a wet tabby cat exactly what she'd been asking for.

Smiling, he tipped back his chair and put his feet up on his desk.

The mere thought of the Anderson babe cooling her heels on the unemployment line was enough to make his day.

CHAPTER TWO

DANA was neck-deep in work.

Unfortunately, none of it was hers. She was too busy fixing up Dave's disasters to pay any attention to her own stuff.

Her tiny cubicle was crowded with files, and her desk was strewn with papers. Memos fought for space with a clutter of computer disks and Styrofoam cups. "The Neat Freak," Dave had dubbed her long before he'd gotten his promotion, but neatness had gone the way of the dodo bird. How could you be neat, when the world was crashing down around your ears?

She'd spent the past hour hunched over the keyboard, hoping to find a way to debug the latest problem in the code. Dana's fingers raced across the keyboard. Numbers scrolled down the screen of her monitor. She paused, scanned the numbers, then hit the "enter" key.

"Please," she said under her breath, "let it be right."

It wasn't.

Not that she'd expected it would be. Mistakes, not miracles, were too often the inevitable result in the wonderful world of computing.

If only Griffin McKenna could get that through his thick skull....

His thick, handsome skull.

Dana muttered a word McKenna surely wouldn't have approved hearing a woman say. She glared at the monitor. Then she sighed, sat back and reached for the closest Styrofoam cup. An inch of black sludge sloshed in the cup's bottom. She made a face, held her breath, and glugged it down. After a minute, she looked at the monitor again.

McKenna's face, complete with its smug, self-confident smirk, seemed to flicker like a ghostly apparition on the screen.

"That's right," she said. "Smile, McKenna. Why wouldn't you? The world is your oyster." Angrily, she tapped the keys again, deleting the numbers, but McKenna's image still lingered. "I should have quit," she muttered. "I should have told that man exactly what he can do with this job."

It wasn't too late. She could pick up the phone, dial his office...

She was reaching for the receiver when the phone rang.

"Hello," she snarled.

"Dana?"

It was Arthur. Dana shut her eyes.

"Oh," she said. "It's you."

"Were you expecting someone else, my dear?"

Dana shot a glance at the monitor, as if she half expected to find McKenna's face still etched onto the glass.

"No," she said. "No, not at all. I just—I'm, ah, I'm awfully busy just now, Arthur, so if you wouldn't mind—"

"Of course, Dana. I only wanted to say hello."

"Hello, then," she said, trying not to sound brusque, "and now, if you'll excuse me..."

"Will I see you this evening?"

"No," she said. "I mean, yes. I mean..."

Dammit. She was being rude, and she was babbling, and it was all because of McKenna. She flashed another quick look at the screen. He was still there, smirking. She stuck out her tongue, then rolled her eyes. What had happened to the rational thought process she was so proud of?

"Arthur." She took a deep breath. "Are you free for lunch? Because if you are, could you meet me at..." Dana paused and did a mental run-through of the restaurants between Arthur's office and hers. McKenna might eat in any one of them, and he was the last person she wanted to see right now. "At Portofino," she said, plucking the name out of the air. It was a name she recalled from a recent review in the *Times*.

"Portofino. Of course. But...all you all right, Dana?"

"I'm fine. It's just... It's just that I need you."

"Oh, my dear," Arthur said, and she didn't realize he might

have gotten the wrong impression until she was on her way out the door.

But by then, it was too late.

Griffin had been in a lot of restaurants in his life, but never in one that reminded him of a chapel.

If only he'd been paying attention when Cynthia had turned up unexpectedly at his office, smiling her perfect smile, looking as if she'd just stepped out of a bandbox—whatever the hell that might be—asking if he'd like to join her for lunch.

Sure, he'd said, even though he knew he should have come up with some excuse because Cynthia was beginning to push things a little too hard. But his thoughts had been on Dana Anderson, and how much pleasure there'd be in firing her, and the next thing he'd known, he and Cynthia had been standing inside this super-trendy, self-conscious watering hole where violins violined and trysters trysted.

"What *is* this place?" he'd muttered.

"It's called Portofino," Cynthia had whispered, giving him a tremulous smile. "Your mother said the *Times* gave it a terrific write-up."

My mother, the matchmaker, Griffin had thought grimly, but he'd managed to smile. Apparently, it was time for another little chat. Marilyn McKenna was wise, sophisticated and charming...but she never gave up. She had decided, a couple of years before, that it was time he married and settled down, and she'd switched her considerable energies from her newest charity to getting him to do just that. Poor Cynthia didn't know it, but she was his mother's latest attempt at moving him toward the goal.

"If you'd rather go someplace else," Cynthia had said, her perfect smile trembling just a little...

"No," Griffin had said, because that was exactly what'd he been thinking. "No, this is fine."

It wasn't fine. The *Times* might love Portofino but as far as he was concerned, the place was a total loser. He liked being able to identify the food on his plate, something you could not

do in the artificial twilight of the restaurant, and if the captain
or the *sommelier* or the waiter slid by one more time, smiling
with oily deference and asking, *sotto voce,* if everything were
all right, he was going to say no, by God, it wasn't, and would
somebody please turn up the lights, dump half the bordelaise
sauce off what might yet prove to be a slab of rare roast beef,
and take away these flowers before he started listening for a
Bach fugue to come drifting from the kitchen?

Griffin smothered a sigh. The truth was that he'd do no such
thing. He'd come here of his own free will, which made paying
the consequences for his stupidity an obligation.

The captain had seated them at a table for two behind the
perfect fronds of an artificial palm tree. The fronds had dipped
into his soup and his salad. Now, they were dipping into his
beef.

"Isn't this romantic?" Cynthia sighed.

"Yes," Griffin said bravely, brushing aside a frond. "Yes,
it is."

"I just knew you'd like it," Cynthia said, batting her lashes.

He'd never noticed that before, that she batted her lashes.
He'd read the phrase in books but until this moment, he hadn't
thought about what it meant. Blink. Blink, blink. It looked
weird. Did all women do that, to get a man's attention? He
couldn't imagine the Anderson woman doing it. She'd probably never batted a lash in her life.

"Griffin?"

Griffin looked up. Cynthia was smiling at him. Nothing new
there; she almost always smiled at him. Not like the charming
Ms. Anderson, who always glared.

"Griffin." Cynthia gave a tinkling little laugh and cocked
her head at a pretty angle. "You seem to be a million miles
away."

"I'm sorry, Cyn." Griffin cleared his throat. "I, ah, I keep
thinking about that conference."

"The one in Florida? Your mother mentioned it."

Give me a break, Mother!

"Yes," he said pleasantly. "It should be interesting. I've never been to a software convention before."

"I envy you," Cynthia said, and sighed.

Griffin's dark brows angled upward. "I didn't know you were interested in computers."

She laughed gaily. "Oh, Griffin! Aren't you amusing? I meant that I envied you for getting away from this cold weather to spend a long weekend in Florida. I only wish I had that opportunity."

Griffin's jaw clenched. Marilyn the Matchmaker was really pushing it this time.

"Yes," he said politely, "I suppose it sounds terrific, but I doubt if I'll even get to set foot on the sand. I'll be too busy rushing from meeting to meeting."

"Ah," Cynthia gazed down at her plate. "I see."

Griffin sighed. No. She didn't see. She was a nice girl, but she was wasting her time. Sooner or later, he was going to have to find a way to tell her that.

It was true, she would undoubtedly make some man a fine wife. She was pretty. Actually, she was beautiful. She was well-educated, too, but she wasn't the kind of woman who was bothered by the fact that she *was* a woman; she understood that there was a difference between the sexes. Griffin had had enough of male-bashing broads to last a lifetime. Any man would, who'd come of age within the past couple of decades.

Cynthia was like a breath of fresh air. She had no agenda and no career goals. She didn't look upon men as the enemy. She liked being a woman. She understood the difference between the sexes, and the difference pleased her.

There was no question as to what would make Cynthia happy. She would be content to be a man's helpmate. To bear his children. To stay at home, cook his meals and clean his house...metaphorically, anyway, because, of course, there'd be a staff of servants to do all of that. The point was, Cynthia would not want the rules bent to accommodate her. She wouldn't leave you wondering if she'd say "thank you" if you opened her car door for her or accuse you of trying to treat her as if she were the weaker sex.

Griffin knew that if he'd been looking for a wife, he'd have looked no further.

But he wasn't looking for a wife. Not yet. Maybe not ever. His life was full and exciting, just the way it was. He loved his work, and his freedom, the right to come and go as he pleased, when he pleased. Not that he didn't enjoy curtailing that freedom from time to time. The world was full of gorgeous women who were eager to share his life for a few weeks or months, no commitments asked. They were not wife material, his mother had said more than once, and each time she did, Griffin nodded thoughtfully and breathed a silent prayer of thanks that they were not.

But—and it was one hell of a big "but"—if he ever did decide it was time to settle down, and if Cynthia was still available, he might just look her up. He liked her well enough; he supposed he could even learn to love her...and if he couldn't imagine taking her in his arms, the way he'd thought about taking Dana Anderson in his arms, and making love on the warm sands of a tropical beach, so what? Wild passion wasn't what married life was all about.

Griffin frowned. Dammit, it wasn't what the Anderson woman was all about, either. Why did he keep thinking about her and that silly beach?

Ms. Anderson, making love on a beach. The very idea was laughable. She'd probably never had a date in her life. She'd probably never...

Griffin jerked back in his seat.

No. It couldn't be!

But it was. There, directly across the restaurant, tucked away in a cozy little nook, sat Dana Anderson...and a man.

What was she doing here? Griffin would have bet anything that she had her lunch in a health food store, or quaffed yogurt at her desk. Instead, here she was amidst the palm fronds and velvet drapes in the pseudo-romantic, sickeningly phony confines of Portofino. And she was with a guy.

An attentive one.

Griffin's frown deepened.

The man could have been chosen for her by central casting. He was perfect, from his tortoise-shells to the bow tie that bobbed on his Adam's apple.

"Monsieur?"

Griffin looked up. The waiter hovered beside the table.

"Do *monsieur* and *madame* wish dessert? A *tarte,* perhaps, or a *Madeline Supreme?"*

What Griffin wanted was to keep watching the Anderson babe and her boyfriend, but Cynthia had that I'm-hurt-but-I'm-being-brave look on her face again. The waiter, who seemed to see nothing strange in a French menu and a French accent in a restaurant named for a town in Portugal and warned, perhaps, by the look on Griffin's face, drew back as if expecting to be attacked.

Griffin did his best to smile politely.

"Nothing for me, thank you," he said. "Cyn? What will you have?"

Cynthia listened attentively while the waiter made his way through a seemingly endless list. Anderson—*Ms.* Anderson—wasn't doing much of anything. She certainly wasn't eating. Griffin couldn't fault her for that. He couldn't see her plate very clearly, thanks to the near-darkness that hung over the room like a pall, but from what he could observe, she was eating what looked like a taxidermist's special.

And the Bow Tie was worried. You could see it on his face. He was looking at Anderson the way a puppy looks at an out-of-reach bone.

Well, who could blame him? Despite the plastered-back hair, the tweed jacket and the loose-fitting twill trousers, Dana Anderson was something to look at.

Griffin frowned. Yeah, well, piranhas were interesting to look at, too.

The guy said something. Anderson started to answer, stopped, then began to speak. She was really getting into it now, gesturing with her hands, leaning forward and risking immolation from the candles flickering in the floral center-piece. She took the guy's hand in hers, and the idiot positively beamed. There was no other way to describe it.

He was smiling so hard it looked as if his ears might start glowing, and why wouldn't he? Anderson was looking at him as if he were St. George standing over the dead body of the dragon when, in reality, the guy looked as if a strong breeze might blow him over.

One corner of Griffin's mouth turned down. This was the Anderson babe's sort of man, all right. A guy she could lead around by the nose. Somebody who'd never want her to dance for him on a deserted stretch of sand, while the moon looked down and the drums pulsed out a beat that matched the fire in his blood...

"Griffin? Griffin, are you all right?"

Griffin pulled back from the edge of the precipice and looked across at Cynthia. "Yes," he said calmly. "Yes, I'm perfectly fine."

And he was.

It was just curiosity that had him wondering what could be keeping Dana Anderson's attention so tightly focused on the man she was with.

"You aren't eating, Dana. Is something wrong with your fish?"

Dana sighed. Arthur was looking at her with concern. Well, no wonder. She'd called and asked him to meet her for lunch, and now she was sitting here like a piece of wood, saying nothing, doing nothing, just watching her own grim reflection in the lenses of his horn-rimmed glasses.

"No," she said, forcing a smile to her lips. "No, the fish is fine, Arthur. Just fine."

It *was* fine. She assumed so, anyway, because the truth was that she hadn't eaten enough of it to know. It was just that Portofino served fish complete with head and tail. The tail didn't bother her but the head was another story. The finny creature lay draped across her plate on a bed of something that looked suspiciously like kelp, its thin mouth turned down, its glassy eye turned up and fixed on the cherubim painted on the gilded ceiling.

Dana repressed a shudder. She'd never been good with food that looked as if it might get up and walk off her plate—or swim off, as the case might be. Besides, if this morning's run-in with McKenna had dimmed her appetite, the atmosphere in Portofino had finished it off completely.

She'd had no idea the place dealt in such overblown decor. If she had, she'd never have suggested it.

No wonder poor Arthur kept looking at her that way, with a little smile on his lips and his gaze expectant and misty behind his horn-rims. Her phone call, her choice of words, even her choice of restaurants, must have convinced him that romance was in the air.

Dana cleared her throat, lay her knife and fork across her plate, and folded her hands in her lap.

"Arthur," she said gently, "I'm afraid I may have misled you."

"I knew it," he said, "you really *don't* like the fish! Where is our waiter? I'll ask him to bring you something else."

Dana sat forward and put her hand on his. "The fish isn't the problem."

Arthur's brows lifted. "It isn't?"

"The problem's..." She frowned. McKenna, was what she'd thought. But what she'd almost said was, me. Me, you, us, Arthur. We're just not right for each other.

But it wasn't true. They *were* right for each other; it was only that she was in an insane mood today. Just look at how she'd treated that poor custodian. She owed him an apology, and she'd give it to him first thing this afternoon, but right now, she was going to let Arthur help her get back on an even track.

He could do it, if anyone could.

"The problem," she said, clearing her throat, "is Griffin McKenna."

Arthur blinked. Just for a moment, it made him bear an uncanny resemblance to her glassy-eyed fish.

"Your employer? My dear Dana, I don't understand. What has he to do with our lunch?"

"Nothing, Arthur. He has to do with me. With my job, with my self-respect, with my responsibilities at Data Bytes." She drew back her hand and sat upright. "You cannot imagine how much I despise that man."

Arthur sighed. "My dear Dana—"

"Do you think you could stop saying that?"

"Saying what, my dear?"

Dana forced a smile to her lips. "Nothing. I'm sorry. I just—I've had a bad morning, that's all. My nerves are shot. That's why I called you. I need your advice."

"You need..." Arthur's smile dimmed just a little, then brightened again. "I'm at your disposal, of course."

"There's a problem at work, with my boss and the code we've been working on. I tried to tell McKenna about it, but he wouldn't listen."

"That's surprising, Dana. Griffin McKenna is a brilliant strategist. According to the *Journal*..."

"The *Journal* doesn't bother mentioning that he's a pompous ass! I hate working for him." Dana paused. "So, I'm asking for your opinion."

Arthur's bow tie rode up and down his Adam's apple. "I'm flattered, my dear."

"Should I start looking for another job?"

"Well, if you ask me—"

"Or should I ride it out? McKenna won't stay at Data Bytes forever, but Dave Forrester probably will."

"True. And—"

"But, if I quit, what kind of references would I get?"

"An excellent ques—"

"On the other hand, what can I accomplish by staying on? Forrester's just going to keep screwing up and McKenna's going to keep treating me as if I'm a troublemaker."

"I see. If you think—"

"He'll fire me anyway, when the new code blows up tomorrow. But if I quit before then, he'll think he forced me out." Dana's eyes narrowed. "I refuse to give him that satisfaction."

"Well," Arthur said quickly, "if you really want my opinion—"

"I might not need references. I know lots of people in this business. I could find a job, a better job, then tell McKenna what he can do with this one!"

"True. But—"

"But that would be giving in. And I won't do that. I'll never do that!" Dana seized Arthur's hand. "Oh, I'm so glad I asked your advice! Thank you for helping me come to a logical decision."

Arthur blinked. "Ah...you're very welcome."

"You're wonderful, you know. You're so clear-headed."

A pink glow suffused Arthur's cheeks. His fingers tightened on hers, and he leaned forward until his bow tie lay nestled among the daisies and tea roses that separated them from each other.

"Thank you, my dear."

"Thank *you*."

Beaming with delight, Arthur lifted her hand to his lips.

"Monsieur." The waiter favored them with the hint of a smile. "Would you and *mademoiselle* care for some *café* and dessert? Some *sorbet,* perhaps, or an excellent *tarte*...''

"Nothing, thank you," Dana said. She smiled at Arthur as she rose to her feet. "I feel rejuvenated, thanks to you, Arthur. And I'm really eager to get back to work."

Cynthia was talking, something about a luncheon she'd attended with his mother. Griffin was trying to pay attention, but how could he, after that incredible display? The Bow Tie had kissed Anderson's hand, and she'd given him a thousand-watt smile in return.

Anderson rose to her feet. So did the Bow Tie. And they headed straight in his direction.

Griffin's jaw tightened. He tossed his napkin on the table and shoved back his chair.

"Griffin?" Cynthia said.

Anderson was holding the guy's arm as they came down the aisle, looking at him as if he were the only man alive.

"Griffin?" Cynthia asked, "are we leaving already?"

Griffin stepped away from the table, folded his arms and waited. The estimable Ms. Anderson was still chattering away, smiling brightly, her head tilted toward the Bow Tie.

Griffin felt a tightness in his belly. She had never looked at him like that. Not that he'd want her to, but still, it was infuriating. She'd given him the kind of look you gave tapioca pudding when you had it shoved in front of you. How come she was gazing at Bow Tie and damn near glowing?

"...Don't know what I'd do without you," she was saying. "You're so good for me."

They were going to walk right into him. Griffin almost smiled as he anticipated her shock. But at the last second, Bow Tie pulled his adoring gaze from Anderson's face, looked up, and saw Griffin standing, immobile, directly in their path.

To say he blanched was to be kind. The guy turned as white as paper.

"Mr. McKenna!"

Anderson nodded. "That's right," she said. "That's all you hear around the office. Mr. McKenna this and Mr. McKenna that, spoken in such hushed tones that, frankly, sometimes I just want to—"

"Now, now," Griffin said coolly. His lips curved into a tight smile as she skidded to a dead stop not more than six inches off his chest. "Be careful what you say, Ms. Anderson. We're in a public place, after all."

Dana's heart slammed into her throat. "You," she croaked as she looked into the scowling face towering above her.

"Indeed, Ms. Anderson. What a small world."

Dana's thoughts were whirling. McKenna? And a woman who looked as if she'd just stepped out of the fashion pages?

But that was impossible. She'd chosen this restaurant with such care! McKenna wasn't supposed to be here.

And why didn't he step back? Why didn't *Arthur* step back? Then, at least, she'd have room to breathe. She wouldn't have to stand so close to McKenna's hard body that she had to tilt her head at a neck-breaking angle just so she could look him in the eye.

"Introduce us," Arthur hissed in her ear.

"Did you enjoy your meal, *Ms.* Anderson?"

"Dana," Arthur whispered, "please. Intro—"

"What are you doing here?" Dana said.

Griffin's scowl deepened. "Having lunch, Ms. Anderson. And you?"

"I don't mean *what* are you doing here, Mr. McKenna, I mean..." God! What *did* she mean? Dana straightened her shoulders. "Excuse me," she said coldly, "but I'd like to get by."

"Oh, I'm sure you would."

"Mr. McKenna. I am on my lunch hour."

McKenna's brows rose. "Is that a fact," he said pleasantly. *Dammit all, why didn't Arthur step back and give her some room?* Dana shoved her elbow into Arthur's middle and shot him an angry look, but he didn't notice. How could he, when he was staring at Griffin McKenna with the look of a deer caught in the headlights?

Dana firmed her jaw, stepped back and planted her foot firmly on Arthur's toes. That made him move, all right, not much but enough so that now she didn't have to inhale faint whiffs of McKenna's cologne with every breath she took.

"It is," she said. "And now, if you'll excuse us, Mr. McKenna, I'll see you back at the office."

Griffin nodded. "Indeed you shall, Miss—oh, sorry—*Ms.* Anderson."

How could the man make the correction of her name sound like an insult? Dana's cheeks burned as she maneuvered past him and headed for the door.

Arthur stepped in front of her when they reached the sidewalk.

"Why didn't you introduce me, Dana?"

She glared past him, at the restaurant, as if McKenna might materialize at any moment.

"The nerve of him," she said, "the damned nerve!"

"You should have introduced us. It was a wonderful oppor—"

"Did you see him? Did you *see* him?"

"Of course, I saw him."

"Don't be dense, Arthur. I mean, did you *see* him? The way he stood there, with that look on his face!"

"What must he be thinking? Common courtesy demands—"

"Courtesy is uncommon, Arthur, haven't you figured that out yet?" Dana blew a strand of streaky blond hair out of her eyes. "And that woman with him. Miss Perfection."

"Actually, I thought she was rather attrac—"

"The polite little smile. The perfect hair. The elegant suit. The la-di-da air."

Arthur frowned in bewilderment. "La-di-da air?"

"So ladylike. So unruffled. So—so unthreatening, to the master's masculinity!"

"Dana, really, I fail to see what you're so upset about."

"That's just the point, Arthur. You fail to see, but that's because...because..."

Because what? What *was* she so upset about? McKenna had been in the same restaurant as she'd been, he'd been having lunch with a beautiful woman. So what?

"If I have to explain it," she said loftily, "there's no point. Goodbye, Arthur. Thank you for lunch."

She swept past him, chin lifted, and started toward the corner. Arthur stared after her for a couple of seconds before hurrying to catch up.

"Dana, my dear, let's not quarrel."

"We haven't quarreled. I just don't see how you can let yourself be taken in by Griffin McKenna."

"I haven't been taken in. I just..." Arthur sighed. "Never mind. Are we still on for dinner this evening?"

"Yes. No. I'm not sure. Why don't you phone me later?"

"Dinner," Arthur said more firmly than usual. "All right?"

Dana sighed. "All right," she said. "I'll see you at seven."

Dave Forrester, who had not yet succumbed to his afternoon ration of vodka, was lounging in the doorway to Dana's office when she returned. He greeted her with an enigmatic look.

"Had a good lunch, did you, Dana?"

"What's that supposed to mean?"

Forrester grinned. "Boss wants to see you."

Dana didn't reply. She turned and walked down the hall to McKenna's office, telling herself as she did that she was not about to take any more nonsense from the man and telling herself, too, that it was a good thing she'd spoken with Arthur because now she was calm, she was very calm, and nothing Griffin McKenna did or said could get under her skin anymore.

Miss Macy greeted her with a look that mimicked Forrester's. Were enigmatic looks the order of the day?

"Mr. McKenna is waiting for you, Miss Anderson."

"It's Ms.," Dana said, and stepped into McKenna's office. He was sitting behind his desk, looking the length of the room at her, like an emperor on his throne. "You wanted to see me, Mr. McKenna?"

"Shut the door please, Ms. Anderson."

Dana complied, then faced him again. "Mr. McKenna. If this is about our bumping into each other at that restaurant—"

"Where you eat is no concern of mine. You may eat what you wish, where you wish, with whomever you wish."

"How generous of you, sir," Dana smiled sweetly. "In that case, what did you want to see me about?"

McKenna smiled, too, like a cat contemplating a cageful of canaries.

"You're fired."

"I beg your pardon?"

"Fired, Ms. Anderson. As in, clean out your desk, collect your severance pay, and don't come back."

Fired? *Fired?* Dana's vision blurred. All the logic of the last hour fled in the face of Griffin McKenna's self-indulgent smile.

"You can't fire me," she snapped. "I quit!"

Griffin tilted back his chair and laced his hands behind his head.

"Have it your way, Ms. Anderson. Frankly, I don't give a damn, just as long as we agree that you are no longer in my employ."

Maybe it was the way he said it, in that know-it-all, holier-than-thou tone. Maybe it was the insufferable smile, or the way he tilted back that damn chair. All Dana knew was that, suddenly, she'd reached the breaking point.

She stomped across the room, snatched a stack of papers from his desk, and flung them high into the air.

"You," she said, "are a complete, absolute, unmitigated jerk."

Griffin looked at Dana. She was breathing as hard as if she'd just finished a five-mile run. Her eyes blazed with green fire, and she looked as if she could happily kill him.

Something in his belly knotted. Slowly, his eyes never leaving hers, he kicked back his chair, rose to his feet and came around the desk.

"And you," he said, "are a woman in need of a lesson."

"In what?" Dana said furiously. "In the fact that the world is owned by men like you?"

A dangerous smile curved across Griffin's mouth. For the second time in her life, and the second time that afternoon, Dana wanted to step back. But she didn't. To give way would have been a mistake.

Standing her ground turned out to be the bigger mistake. It meant that when Griffin reached for her, he had no trouble pulling her straight into his arms.

"In the fact that women have their uses, Ms. Anderson," he said, and then he bent his head, laced his fingers into her hair, and kissed her.

CHAPTER THREE

IT WASN'T much of a kiss, as kisses went.

No bells. No fireworks. No explosion of colors behind Dana's closed eyelids.

Not that she'd deliberately shut her eyes. It had been reflex, that was all. And she certainly hadn't expected bells or fireworks. That was the stuff of women's novels, those silly books that were all fantasy.

It was only that somehow, when a man like Griffin McKenna kissed you, you thought—you sort of assumed—dammit, you *expected*...

Expected?

She *hadn't* expected. That was just the point. McKenna had hauled her into his arms and sent her straight into shock. And that, plain and simple, was what he'd counted on.

Dana exploded into action, twisting free of McKenna's grasp, balling her hand into a fist and whamming it into his middle. It was like pounding her knuckles against a rock but it was worth it. Oh, yes, it certainly was, just to see the look of astonishment spread across that too-handsome-for-its-own-good face.

"Hey," he said, sounding indignant.

Dana's blood pressure soared.

"Hey? *Hey?*" She jabbed her forefinger into his chest. It was steely, too, like his middle, so she jabbed again, a lot harder. "Is that all you have to say for yourself, you—you beetle-browed Neanderthal?"

"Now, wait just a—"

"How dare you, McKenna? How *dare* you kiss me?"

She paused for breath and Griffin opened his mouth, determined to get a word in while he could...and then he shut it again. She was waiting for an answer. She *deserved* an answer. Unfortunately, he didn't have one.

Why *had* he kissed her? It was an excellent question. She'd stood there, glowering at him, drawing a line in the dust, so to speak, women on one side, men on the other. So what? You didn't kiss a woman because she didn't like men. You didn't look at the sexual chip on her shoulder and see it as a dare.

On the other hand, that was damn well what it was. And facing down dares had been the story of his life, starting with the day he'd inherited his father's fortune along with a note handed over by John McKenna's embarrassed attorney, a note that had contained a line he'd never forget.

Here's my fortune, Griffin, his father had written. *I worked a lifetime to build it. How long will you take to waste it?*

That challenge, even though it had been given by a man who'd never had time for his wife or son, had driven a knife into Griffin's heart. But he'd risen to it, perhaps beyond it, and built an empire he was proud of, one that might even have impressed his father.

But what kind of dare was there in hauling an unwilling woman into your arms?

None. Absolutely none whatsoever. So, why had he done it?

Griffin frowned. Damned if he could come up with a reason. A lesson, he'd said, but what lesson? Not even he believed in all that old crap he'd spouted about a woman's place being in the kitchen and in the bedroom.

Okay, so he didn't like the kind of female who saw men as the enemy. Who eagerly awaited the day they could reproduce by cloning and let the opposite sex kill themselves off, trying to gather a harem.

That didn't mean he belonged to the "knock 'em in the head, toss 'em over your shoulder, drag 'em off to the cave" crowd, either—and yet, how else could you describe what he'd just done?

"Your silence is eloquent, McKenna."

Griffin focused on Dana's face, still flushed with anger.

"I take it to mean that even *you* are aware that the days are long gone when a man could get away with coming on to a woman as if they were both decked out in animal skins!"

Griffin's frown deepened. She was right, that was the damnedest part. It was what had kept him from *really* kissing her, the sudden realization, once he'd had her in his arms, that there was absolutely no rational explanation for what he was doing, that the "Me man, you woman" thing had never held any appeal for him.

By God, much as he hated to admit it, he owed her an apology.

He cleared his throat.

"Miss Anderson—"

"*Ms.,*" she said, her tone frigid enough to freeze water. "Or are you memory-impaired, as well as hormonally imbalanced?"

A muscle ticked in Griffin's jaw. "Ms. Anderson," he said, telling himself to stay calm, "I suppose I— I mean, I guess, maybe—"

He couldn't say it. Why should he apologize, when she was glowering at him as if he were something that had just crawled out from under a rock?

Because it's the right thing to do, McKenna, that's why.

Hell, he thought, and he thrust his hand into his hair, shoving the dark locks back from his forehead, and told himself to try again.

"Listen," he said. "Listen, Ms. Anderson—"

"No," Her eyes, those green, green eyes that could be so filled with heat one second and so icy cold the next, fixed on his. "No," she repeated, punctuating each word with a poke to his sternum, "*you* listen, Mr. McKenna!"

Griffin caught hold of Dana's wrist. "Ms. Anderson, if you'd just calm down—"

"Unhand me, Mr. McKenna!"

Unhand me? Griffin stifled a chuckle. It didn't take a genius to know that laughter would only make her more furious, but hell, *unhand me...*

"I said…"

"I heard you," He let go of her wrist, screwed his face into an expression he hoped would communicate apology, and started over. "Ms. Anderson, I'd like to tell you—"

"I'm not the least bit interested in anything you have to say, McKenna—but you might be interested in what *I* have to tell *you*," She smiled, put her hands on her hips, and tilted back her head so that their eyes met. "In fact, I'm certain of it. It's going to wipe that—that stupid grin right off your face!"

"Ms. Anderson. I can assure you, I am not grinning. I am not even smiling. If you'd just keep quiet for a minute and let me talk—"

Her index finger made another dent in the front of his shirt.

"Your lawyers will have to do the talking, because I, Mr. McKenna, am going to see to it that every woman in New York knows exactly what kind of man you are!"

Griffin's eyes narrowed. "Stop poking at me."

"Did you hear what I said? I'm going to sue the pants off you!"

His hand clamped down on hers. "Did you hear what *I* said, Anderson? I am not a human pincushion!"

"Let go of me!"

"When you calm down, I'll let go."

"I am calm. Completely calm. Calm enough to assure you that the Griffin McKenna who—who swashes his way through life is in deep trouble."

"Swashes?" Griffin couldn't help it. This time, he did laugh. "What in hell does that mean?"

"Go ahead. Laugh. Laugh all the way to court because you'll never laugh again, after I get done suing you for sexual harassment."

"You're joking."

"Do I look as if I'm joking?"

Griffin considered. What she looked was furious. Indignant. Righteous…and out and out gorgeous. He could feel her pulse leaping just under the soft skin at her wrist. Her eyes were the color of the Atlantic off Cape Cod, just before a storm. Her cheeks were the tender color of new roses. And, somehow or other, her hair had come undone.

Somehow or other? His body tightened. Why was he being so modest? He knew how her hair had come undone. He had done it, plunging his hands into it when he'd kissed her.

But he hadn't kissed her. Not really. The thought had been there, even the intention, but before he'd had time to get started, the knowledge of exactly what he was doing had broken through his anger and he'd clamped down on the kiss so that it had been nothing more than a touch of his mouth against hers.

If he'd kissed her, really kissed her, it would have been more than that. He'd have drawn her close against his body, held her so that he could feel the softness of her breasts against his chest. He'd have parted her lips with his, tasted all the heat bottled inside her, savored the silkiness of her mouth—that soft-looking, sweet mouth. He'd have inhaled her scent, whispered her name, accepted her surrender as she wound her arms around his neck....

"—anything to say?"

Griffin blinked and let go of her hand. "What?"

"For a man who's always barking orders, you don't seem to have much to say right now." Dana glared. "Maybe you think I'm joking about slapping you with a lawsuit for sexual harassment!"

"Look, Anderson, if you want an apology—"

"An apology?" Dana said in a way that made his hackles rise. "You've got to be joking. What I want is your neck in the noose of the law," She shot him a smile that would have bared her fangs, if she'd had any. "And believe me, that's just what I'm going to do. I am going to sue you for every cent you've got, McKenna. And when I'm done, the entire world will know just what a sexist rat fink you are."

Gorgeous, but nuts, Griffin thought, and folded his arms over his chest.

"Listen here, lady—"

"I am not a lady!"

"Damn right, you aren't."

"Don't twist my words, McKenna! You know what I mean. I am *not* a lady, I am a human being. A person. And I don't have to take any nonsense from the likes of you."

"If you'd just shut up for two minutes, you'd know that I've been trying to apologize."

"For what?"

"For kissing you, that's for what."

"It's too late. You've already done it."

Griffin swore. "Of course, I've already done it! How in hell could I apologize if I..." He stopped, counted silently to five, and tried again. "Look, let's not make a mountain out of a molehill."

Dana folded her arms, too. "You're the mole who's building the mountain, not me."

"Okay. Okay, you want to sue me?" Griffin glared at her. "Sue me, then."

"I intend to."

"Assuming, that is, you can find some shyster lawyer to take the case."

"Any lawyer worth her salt will jump at the chance, McKenna."

"Any lawyer with half a brain will burst your bubble, Anderson." He smiled smugly. "You can't sue me."

"Says who?"

"Says logic. You don't work for me anymore, remember?"

Was he right? Dana felt a moment's panic. She couldn't let him get away with what he'd done...or with that one instant when she'd wished he'd done more.

"That has nothing to do with it," she said. "This is America. I can sue anybody I want to sue."

"Dammit, don't wag your finger in my face!"

"I'll wag it anywhere I choose. I don't work for you anymore, as you so generously pointed out. I don't have to take orders."

"You're right," he said grimly. "You don't have to take orders. And I don't have to be polite."

"Polite? You?" Dana laughed. "You wouldn't know how to be polite if Emily Post gave you private lessons!"

"Emily Post is dead!"

"Your reputation will be, too, when I'm done with my lawsuit!"

"Do you ever step down from that soapbox, Anderson?"

"What soapbox?"

"The one marked 'neuter' where it says 'gender.'"

"That's pathetic, McKenna."

"It's the truth. Forrester was right about you."

"Forrester?" Dana frowned. "What does he have to do with this?"

"He tried telling me what you were, from day one. He said you were a frustrated broad who hated all men as a matter of principle."

Dana's face flushed crimson with anger. "I won't even justify that with a response."

"Why? Does it hit too close to home?"

"Step into the twenty-first century, McKenna. Women who choose careers over marriage are not frustrated."

Griffin smiled coldly. "Got a torrid thing going with the Bow Tie, do you?"

"You are truly pathetic!"

"I'm a man, is what you mean."

"You're an anachronism, and since there are too many syllables in that word for you to understand it, let me explain it to you."

"Oh, by all means, Anderson. Please do."

"You, Mr. McKenna, are a man who still thinks a woman's place is in the home."

Griffin looked at Dana. Her hair, so neatly arranged until he'd touched it, flew wildly about her flushed cheeks. Anger had put glints of fire in her eyes, and her breath was coming so fast that not even the dowdy blouse and tailored jacket could disguise the upthrust roundness of her breasts.

Something dark and dangerous seemed to uncoil deep within him. Don't, a voice inside him warned. But Griffin was a man who'd never refused a challenge, especially one he'd imposed on himself.

"You're wrong," he said in a tone as cold as his blood was hot. "I've always known exactly where women really belong."

He reached out, tugged her into his arms, and kissed her again.

It was nothing like the kiss of minutes ago.

That was Dana's first thought.

Her second was that New York had to be undergoing an earthquake, because she could feel the floor tilt beneath her feet.

His mouth had been cool when he'd kissed her before. Now it was hot. Hot, and hard—though, even as she thought it, his lips softened, shaped hers, and opened her to him.

The rotten bastard, she thought...and then, with absolutely no warning, she was tumbling into heat and darkness, the floor was not just tilting, it was turning, and the only thing she could do was curl her fingers into the lapels of Griffin's jacket and hang on.

Someone made a soft, moaning sound. Was it she? It had to be, because Griffin wasn't moaning. He was making a low sound in the back of his throat, something between a growl and a purr. And he was drawing her closer against him, holding her tightly in his arms, so that their bodies were meshed, breast to breast, belly to belly, toe to toe.

His hands swept down her back, cupped her bottom and lifted her against him. She felt the hardness of his erection press against her.

What am I doing? she thought crazily, and she lifted her arms and wound them tightly around Griffin's neck. Her fingers plunged into his hair; her breath quickened. She whimpered as his teeth closed lightly on her bottom lip, as he sucked the tender flesh into the heat of his mouth...

And then, as suddenly as he'd taken her in his arms, Griffin cupped her elbows, put her away from him, and stepped back.

Dana swayed, blinked her eyes open—and looked straight into his expressionless face.

"You see?" he said very calmly. "Women do have their uses."

"What?" she said in a hoarse whisper.

"I said, you have no case, Ms. Anderson."

"No..." Dana swallowed dryly. "No case?"

Griffin's smile crooked at the corner of his mouth. He rocked back on his heels and tucked his hands into his trouser pockets.

"None at all. Unless, of course, you're prepared to have me describe, in excruciating detail, every last second of our little encounter."

Dana put her hand to her throat. "You mean—you mean, you deliberately..."

"Did you think I was overwhelmed by passion, Ms. Anderson?" The arrogant smile became an egotistical grin. "Perhaps I should refresh your memory. You sighed. You moaned. You—"

Color flamed in her face. "I did not!"

"Moaned," he said pleasantly. "And you damn near strangled me when you wrapped your arms around my neck."

"You rat! You swine! You no good—"

"And then, of course, there's the way you opened your mouth. And kissed me back. Very effective move, Ms. Anderson. And nicely done."

"You—you—you—"

He caught her wrist as her hand flew toward him, and drew it down to her side.

"Think about it," he said softly. The smile was gone from his face now. In its place was a look so cold it made Dana's breath catch. "Do you really want to pursue a lawsuit that will only prove my point?"

"What point?" Dana said, her voice trembling with anger. "That you're detestable?"

"That you're exactly what I said you were, Anderson. A

frustrated female, in desperate need of..." He paused delicately. "...Male attention."

She struggled, desperately, to control herself. She knew what he wanted, that she should weep or rage or do whatever he thought women were supposed to do when things went against them. In his mind, she'd already become a stereotype. She'd behaved as he'd expected because, somehow, he'd managed to put her off balance more times than she'd have thought possible.

But it wouldn't happen again. Women—strong, independent women—should always be in firm control of themselves, and of their destinies. Hadn't she learned that in childhood, watching her mother tolerate her stepfather's ugly domination? Dana had vowed, years ago, that she would never bend to any man's will.

But she'd bent to this man. He'd gotten her to lose her composure. Her sanity. Why else would she have returned his kiss? And that was what she'd done; there was no sense lying to herself about it.

How could she have done that? How *could* she?

"Nothing to say, *Ms.* Anderson?"

His tone mocked her. Dana stiffened and looked into that handsome, self-assured face.

"Nothing at all," she said calmly. "Except that if I ever have the misfortune to set eyes on you again, Mr. McKenna, I won't hesitate to wrap a crowbar around your thick skull."

Griffin turned his back and strolled to his desk. "I'll be sure never to give you the opportunity. Now, if we're finished here, I'll phone Payroll and have them draw your check."

"Be sure to include the three weeks severance pay that I'm entitled to."

He glanced up. It pleased her to see a glimmer of surprise in his eyes.

"I'll do that."

Dana nodded. She turned briskly and walked to the door. At the last second, hand on the knob, she looked back. McKenna, seated behind his desk, had already put her out of his mind. He was concentrating on a paper in front of him, frowning and making quick notes on it with his pen.

"McKenna?" He looked up, and she smiled tightly. "Just for the record..."

"Yes?"

"That moan you thought you heard?" Her smile widened until it glittered. "Actually, it was me, trying not to retch. I guess we're both fortunate that you let me go when you did."

It wasn't much, as curtain lines went, she thought as she slammed the door and marched past a startled Miss Macy. But anything was better than letting Griffin McKenna think his kiss had affected her. It was the suddenness of it that had affected her, that, and all the emotional ups and downs of the last few weeks.

Why hadn't she realized that so she could have told him so a few minutes ago, when he was standing there and gloating?

Not that it mattered. She had seen the last of Mighty McKenna.

"Goodbye, and good riddance," she muttered, and she picked up her pace and headed down the hall to Payroll.

Safe inside his office, Griffin let out his breath as the door slammed shut.

He put down the paper he'd pretended to read, tossed aside his pen, and ran his fingers through his hair.

What had gotten into him?

Kissing Anderson once had been stupid, but kissing her twice? That had been insane. She hadn't wanted him to kiss her, and he was not a man whose ego was so big that it kept him from understanding that when a woman said "no," "no" was what she meant.

Besides, he didn't even like Dana Anderson.

Griffin shoved back his chair and got to his feet. Didn't like her? He almost laughed as he stood at the window, staring down into the canyon of skyscrapers around him. That had to be the understatement of the year. The redoubtable Ms. Anderson would never, not in a lifetime, make it onto a list of women he'd hope to be stranded with on a deserted island, not even if every female on the planet suddenly vanished, except for her.

So, how come he'd kissed her the second time? How come that second kiss had left him feeling as if all the air had been sucked out of his lungs? And when she'd risen up on her toes, looped those slender arms around his neck...when she'd done that, what little remained of his control had all but fled. He'd wanted to carry Dana Anderson to the sofa, lay her down upon it and make love to her until neither of them had the strength to move.

Griffin shuddered. At least he'd come to his senses in time. He'd been a breath away from tearing off her clothes—and she'd have let him, he knew that as surely as he knew his own name—when his brain had said "hello" and his hormones had said "goodbye." He'd shoved her away, come up with an explanation fast enough to make his head spin, and then he'd had to climb out of the hole he'd been busily digging under his own feet.

"Damn," Griffin said softly, and shook his head.

"Sir?"

He swung around. Miss Macy was standing in the doorway, her bushy brows raised in inquiry.

"I knocked, sir, but—"

"What is it, Miss Macy?"

"Payroll telephoned, sir. Miss Anderson is there, asking about a check."

"Yes," he said briskly, "that's correct. Miss Anderson's been terminated. Tell Payroll I said they're to write her a check for the week, and to include whatever severance pay she's entitled to."

"Certainly, Mr. McKenna. Will that be all?"

No, Griffin thought. Get me the number of a good psychiatrist.

"Yes," he said, "thank you, Miss Macy. That will be all."

The dragon turned, hurried to the door, then paused and looked back at him.

"Oh, Mr. McKenna? I have those documents ready for you, sir. Do you want to go through them, or shall I put them into your attaché case?"

Griffin tried to figure out what in hell she was talking about, and failed.

"Documents?"

"Yes, sir. For your trip to Florida tomorrow. The work-ups, the specification sheets... Did you want to see them again?"

Florida. Tomorrow. Griffin almost groaned. He'd managed to forget all about the convention, the appointments, and the new program—a program that was still flawed, thanks to the bumbling efforts of the charming Ms. Anderson.

"Sir?"

"I suppose I'd better take one last look, Miss Macy. Yes, please, bring me the papers. And phone Dave Forrester. Tell him I'd like to see him ASAP."

Moments later, Griffin was elbow-deep in printouts of what might as well have been gibberish. After a while, he shoved everything aside and massaged his temples with the tips of his fingers.

Who was he kidding? Reading this stuff was like reading Sanskrit. He knew how to use computers, not how to program them. He'd just have to rely on Dave's expertise. He'd have to rely on him for a lot of things, if this program wasn't up and running by tonight, which was just one more thing to lay in Dana Anderson's lap.

It was too damn bad he hadn't fired her the minute Dave had launched his first complaint.

Griffin frowned and looked at his watch. Where was Forrester, anyway?

Leaning forward, he hit a button on his telephone.

"Miss Macy," he said. "Would you please ring Dave Forrester again, and—"

The door swung open. Griffin looked up. Miss Macy looked back at him, her hands clasped tightly against her flat bosom.

"Mr. McKenna," she gasped, "I tried to stop him, sir, but—"

A man shoved past her. Griffin rose to his feet.

"Dave?" he said.

It was Dave, all right, but a Dave he'd never seen before. Forrester's eyes were red and shiny, he had a stain down the front of his shirt, and he was wearing a big, loopy grin.

"Dave?" Griffin said again, "what is this?"

"You fired her," Forrester said, listing to the right.

Griffin nodded. "Anderson? Yeah. I did. I just wish I'd listened to you all along and... What's going on here, Dave? Are you sick?"

"I'm fine. I'm A-OK, ol' buddy," Dave grinned again and listed to the left. Griffin hurried forward and grabbed his arm. "Good riddance to bad rubbish, is what I say, ya know?"

"Dave," Griffin said cautiously, "come and sit down. Miss Macy? I wonder if you might check and see if there's a doctor in the building."

"I doan need a doctor," Forrester said, and hiccuped.

It was the hiccup that did it. Griffin drew back, grimacing. "Dammit, Forrester, you smell like a brewery!"

"A distill'ry," Forrester said, and chuckled. "'At's twelve-year-old Scotch, Griff, old man." He winked and leaned in close. "Ran outta vodka a li'l while ago. Wouldn't put it past that busybody to have stolen my stash 'n tossed it out."

"Busybody?" Griffin said, trying not to inhale as he half dragged Forrester toward the sofa.

"The Anderson broad. She's always pokin' her nose where it doesn't belong."

Griffin felt himself grow cold. "She said you were a drunk," he said, looking at his old friend. "And I didn't believe her."

"Me? A drunk? Doan be sil..."

Forrester groaned. His eyes rolled up in his head and he tumbled, backward, onto the cushions.

CHAPTER FOUR

DANA phoned Arthur from the lobby of the Data Bytes building.

He was in a meeting, his secretary said, but if it was urgent...

Urgent? Dana almost laughed. She'd lost her job, been humiliated...

"Ms. Anderson? Is it urgent? Because if it is, I can beep him for you."

"No," Dana said quickly. "No, it isn't urgent. Not at all. Just tell Mr. Coakley that I phoned, please, about our dinner appointment, and—"

"Oh, that reminds me. Mr. Coakley asked me to phone *you* and say that he's made reservations for six o'clock, at someplace called The Arbor. It's on—"

"I know where it is, Ms. Costello, but I can't—"

"Ms. Anderson, I have a call on another line. Would you mind holding for a moment, please?"

Dana leaned her forehead against the frosted glass partition of the telephone kiosk.

"That's all right," she said wearily. "Just tell Mr. Coakley that I'll see him at six."

She hung up the phone, looked at her watch, and headed for the door. Two hours to kill. Well, that was just as well. She needed time to calm down and collect her thoughts before she met Arthur. Steady, dependable, levelheaded Arthur. He'd help her put things in perspective.

Yes, she thought as she made her way briskly along Madison Avenue, Arthur would get her back on an even keel.

She broke the news to him just after they'd been served their main course.

"Arthur?"

He looked up. Something pink and gelatinous was poised on the tines of his fork.

"Yes, my dear?"

"I quit."

Arthur looked at her untouched plate and frowned. "Without so much as tasting your duck? Really, Dana—"

"My job," she said, her voice steady. "I quit it, this afternoon."

She watched his expression go from puzzlement to disbelief. The forkful of pink stuff slid, unnoticed, to his plate.

"You're joking."

She leaned forward, carefully avoiding the lit tapers in the center of the table. The last time they'd dined here, the décor had been about as romantic as a museum cafeteria. Now, the place seemed to be in a battle with Portofino for the title of Chapel of the Month. What was happening to Manhattan restaurants? she wondered idly. Had they been taken over by flower children from the sixties?

"I wouldn't joke about a thing like that, Arthur."

His face turned pale. "You mean..."

"I mean what I said. I quit."

"Just like that?"

Dana nodded. "Just like that."

She saw his bow tie slide up, then down, as he swallowed. The desire to reach over, rip off the silly tie and toss it away was almost overwhelming.

Stop it, she told herself fiercely. *Whatever is wrong with you, Dana?*

There was no sense letting her anger out on poor Arthur. It wasn't his fault she felt like an overwound spring. She'd walked the afternoon away, but it hadn't done a thing toward easing her anger. She'd have had to fly to one of the islands in the Caribbean to manage that and find a place where she could have had a little wax doll made in Griffin McKenna's smarmy image.

"Oh, my dear," Arthur said. "How did it happen?"

She sighed. Arthur was looking at her as if she'd just told him the world was going to end in twenty-four hours. Of course, now that she'd been fired, now that her employment records undoubtedly said she was a disaster as a programmer, now that she'd joined New York's legion of the unemployed, that might just be the reasonable way to view things.

"How does it usually happen? McKenna called me in to fire me, and—"

"I thought you said you quit."

"Quit, fired...what's the difference? I'm no longer employed at Data Bytes."

"Dana." Arthur cleared his throat. "There's a world of difference. Were you fired, or did you quit?"

"Both," she said after a minute.

"It can't be both."

"Yes, it can."

Arthur frowned. "Let's begin again, Dana. I thought we'd agreed, at lunch, that you would not quit your job."

"We did. And I didn't."

"But you just said—"

"It wasn't my idea, Arthur, but when McKenna told me I was fired, I had to say something, didn't I? So I said he couldn't fire me, that I quit."

Arthur stared at her for a few seconds. "I see."

"You don't."

"I do. You were upset—"

"I was angry."

"Whatever. And so you thought to trump him by quitting."

Dana sighed and picked up her fork. "It was something like that, I guess."

"Well, we'll have to think this through. Surely there's some recourse you can take."

"I am not going to crawl back to the man and beg for my job, Arthur."

"No, of course not. I simply meant that there's surely some positive action to be taken, even in view of the current turn of events."

She looked at him. "Do you really think so?"

"Certainly. We can't simply let this slide by without taking action."

Dana smiled. "Thank you," she said softly. "I wasn't sure you'd see this my way, Arthur."

"Dana, my dear, you know how much you mean to me. Why wouldn't I back you at a moment such as this?"

"Well—well, I know you thought I was crazy for disliking McKenna. I mean, I know you think he's the god of takeovers, or something..."

"He's an acknowledged leader in his field. But that has nothing to do with what he did to you today. The only question is, who made the first move?"

Dana's heart skipped a beat. She saw herself in Griffin McKenna's arms, their mouths fused in passion.

"The first move?" she said in a croaking whisper.

"Yes. Did he make it, or did you?"

"Well—he did, but—"

"Did he give any warning?"

"Warning?"

"That's right. Warning. Some sort of signal, so you could attempt to discourage him?"

"Certainly, I tried to discourage him! If you think I simply let that man—"

"That's what we must determine. Because if he didn't give you any warning, Dana, the situation works to our benefit."

A nervous laugh rose in her throat. "It does?"

"It does, indeed."

"I don't—I don't see how, Arthur. What does it matter? Besides, I know what he'll claim. He'll say that I—that I kissed him back. It isn't true, of course. I mean, it may have seemed... What's the matter?"

"Kissed?" Arthur said. His face had gone white. *"Kissed?"*

"Yes. It wasn't my idea. It was just as you said. McKenna started it, and I..." Dana's eyes widened. "Wasn't that what you were talking about?"

"No." Arthur's voice was wooden. "It was not." He leaned forward, the neat, center knot of his tie bobbing inches above the flickering candles. "Let me understand this. You kissed Griffin McKenna?"

"Yes. No! He kissed me. He..." Dana swallowed hard. What an idiot she was! Of course, Arthur hadn't been referring to that kiss. How could he have been? Only she and the detestable McKenna knew he had kissed her...

...*Knew she had kissed him back*...

"Dana?"

She forced her gaze to focus on Arthur's face. Two red spots had appeared on his cheeks.

"What, precisely, went on in McKenna's office?"

"Nothing that had any meaning. He was angry. I was angry. And things just—they just..." She drew a shuddering breath. "What were you talking about, then? If not—if not... You said it mattered, if I'd tried to stop him. What was that all about?"

Arthur sat back. He took off his glasses, polished them meticulously with his linen napkin, peered through first one lens and then the other, then put the glasses on again. The color in his cheeks had faded to a dull pink and, when he spoke, his tone was calm.

"Unemployment insurance."

Dana blinked. "Unemployment insurance?"

He nodded. "If McKenna fired you without warning you that he was displeased with specific aspects of your performance, you might have a case. But if you quit before he had the chance to say anything, you probably haven't."

"Unemployment insurance," Dana said again. She nodded, put her hands in her lap and linked her fingers tightly together. "Of course."

"I realize the amount you'd get per week isn't huge, but it would help until you found another position."

She nodded. Money. Arthur had been talking about money, and she'd thought... But why wouldn't she have thought? That kiss, that damnable kiss, was stuck in her mind. It had been nothing but deliberate humiliation. Griffin McKenna had wanted to make her look foolish, and he'd succeeded, and now she couldn't stop thinking about it, about how she wished she'd had the presence of mind to have reacted properly, but McKenna had timed the thing well. He'd grabbed her when she'd been in such a state of confusion that she hadn't known what she was doing.

"...phone them on your behalf Monday morning, first thing. If you approve, naturally. Dana? Do you agree?"

"Phone who?"

"Some people I know at Social Services. Haven't you been listening?"

"Of course," she said blithely. "Thank you, Arthur. By all means, phone them. I'd be grateful."

And she would be. Arthur was good, he was kind, he would never treat a woman as Griffin had treated her...

...*Never take her mouth with his and make the earth move beneath her feet...*

Dana pushed back her chair and scrambled to her feet.

"Dana? My dear, what is it?"

"I—I need some air, Arthur. It's so stuffy in here. And—and I've had such a long, miserable day..."

"I understand." Arthur rose, too. He took out his wallet, peeled off some bills, frowned, studied them, looked toward the ceiling as he did a mental count of what they'd ordered and what he owed.

"Sixty should do it," he murmured. He hesitated. "Actually, it should be fifty-eight seventy-five, but—"

Dana bit down on her lip. Griffin McKenna would never be so cautious. Griffin would peel off some bills, toss them down. Actually, he'd never have let things go this far. He'd have sensed her mood the minute he saw her; he'd have swept her into his arms, stroked her hair back from her cheeks, smiled into her eyes and kissed her until her worries were gone, until she could think only of him...

"And we both ordered the chocolate mousse."

"Dammit all, Arthur!" She reached across the table, snatched the bills from under his nose and dumped them on the table. "Just pay the damn thing," she sputtered, and then she grabbed her jacket and her handbag and hurried from the restaurant, with Arthur following in her wake.

People said New York was a city that never slept.

It was the truth. No matter what the hour, day or night, you could find people, shops, businesses ready and willing to serve you.

That was why Dana could sit cross-legged on the floor in her living room at six in the morning with an open box from Picasso's Perfect Pizzas in front of her. There was a can of Diet Coke in her left hand and a half-eaten wedge of sausage, mushroom and onion pizza in her right. She'd already finished two pieces; they lay in her gut with all the delicacy of hippopotamuses tiptoeing through a field of tulips. She could almost feel the weight settling onto her hips.

A string of cheese oozed from the wedge of pizza. Dana tilted it up, slurped at the cheese before it dropped onto her Daffy Duck sweatshirt, chewed and swallowed. Before her, on the flickering television screen, a woman in a thong leotard stretched long, limber muscles in time to a pounding rock beat. Dana assumed that was what it was; she had the sound turned off.

"One, and two, and three," the woman on-screen mouthed.

"One, and two, and three," Dana said around her mouthful of pizza.

"Push, and pull, and breathe in deep," the vision mimed.

"Push, and pull, and, oh...to heck with it!"

Dana swallowed the last bit of pizza, picked up the remote control, and zapped the exercise princess into oblivion. Who could believe that someone who looked like that needed to work herself into a sweat?

"Not me," Dana muttered as she got to her feet.

Exercise had been Arthur's idea. He'd put her into a taxi and told her to go home and not worry about a thing.

"I'm not worried," she'd said, looking at him through the open window as he shut the cab's door. "I'm angry. To think that that man fired me...to think he believed all the garbage Forrester told him..."

"I'll take care of everything," Arthur had said soothingly, and then he'd leaned in, given her a quick kiss, and told her to go home and work off her anger on the Exercycle he'd given her for Christmas, after she'd mentioned she'd been thinking about taking up running.

"You cannot run alone," he'd said. "It isn't safe."

"I know Tai Chi and karate, Arthur. Remember? I told you, I took some classes in college."

Arthur's frown had told her what he thought of such a sweaty sport.

"I'd worry about you, my dear," he'd said. "Really, you shouldn't run by yourself."

She'd thought, just for a minute, that he'd meant he was going to run with her. But he hadn't. Arthur's heart wasn't into sports. Instead, on Christmas morning, a huge box had been delivered to her door. It had contained an Exercycle, but Dana had never used it.

She didn't like it.

Stupid as it was, the machine that sat in the corner of her living room seemed to be a constant reminder of Arthur's pasty-white body. They'd gone to Fire Island for a day, last summer; the sight of Arthur in his black trunks had not been cheering.

For shame, Dana!

Why would he be muscular? she asked herself as she dumped the rest of Picasso's Perfect Pizza into the garbage. Arthur worked with his mind, not with his hands. There was no reason for a man like him to have muscles.

There was no reason for Griffin McKenna to have them, either, but he did. His arms had been hard as steel, as he'd held her, his body against hers as hard as granite. No, not granite. Rock was cold to the touch but Griffin...Griffin was hot.

Dana gave herself a determined shake.

"Idiot," she said.

Briskly, she peeled off Daffy Duck and her sweatpants and headed for the shower.

At seven, she'd exchanged Diet Coke for black coffee, jeans for sweatpants, and Daffy's smiling likeness for that of Lois Lane.

Lois Lane, though still much too dependent on Superman, was the preferable choice this morning.

Dana sipped her coffee. She felt better now, even though she hadn't slept all night. How could she have slept, with the knowledge of her humiliation at McKenna's hands to haunt her?

But it was the dawn of a new day, both literally and figuratively. It was time to put yesterday aside and concentrate on tomorrow.

In other words, she was going to begin the search for a job.

Dana unlocked the door and looked on the mat for the newspaper. It wasn't there. Well, that was no surprise. The *Times* was delivered to her door each morning, but José was sometimes late. Usually, he dropped the paper off at six or seven, but once in a while, it would be later than that because she'd find it on her doorstep when she returned from work in the evening. She didn't have the heart to complain. José was a scruffy-looking kid, in perpetual need of a haircut, and when she'd confronted him about it, he'd told her he had to take care of his mother before he did his route.

His eyes had defied her to argue.

Dana sighed. Why would she have argued? She'd had a mother to take care of, too, and though she had no way of knowing if the situations were similar, she knew how rough it was for a kid to take on such a responsibility.

Okay. She'd go down to the coffee shop on the corner, pick

up the paper, and go through the employment section. There wouldn't be much, not on a Friday, but it would be a start. And then she'd phone Jeannie, who had to be wondering what on earth had happened to her. The rumor mill at Data Bytes would be working overtime by now. Jeannie would have heard a dozen different versions of the firing. It would be vital to make sure the true one found its way into the pipeline.

In fact, she'd phone Jeannie, right now, tell her what had really happened in McKenna's office...

Tell her about that kiss?

Dana froze, portable telephone in hand, but it was too late. She'd already dialed, and Jeannie had picked up.

"Hullo?"

"Uh, it's me. Did I wake you?"

"No," Jeannie said in a sleep-fogged voice.

"I figured you had to be getting up soon, to go to work."

"Right, right. Jus' give me a couple seconds to focus here..."

"No, that's okay. I'll call back when you're—"

"Dana? Dana!" Jeannie's voice sharpened. "It's you!"

Dana ran her hand through her hair. It was still damp from the shower and starting its usual, impossible tendency to curl.

"Yeah. It's me."

"Thank God! I'd begun to think you'd been kidnapped by gypsies or something. I must have phoned you a dozen times last evening. Don't you ever check your answering machine?"

Dana glanced at the machine as she paced past it. Its red light was blinking furiously. Arthur had bought it for her for her birthday, but she still tended to forget its existence.

"Sorry. I didn't mean to worry you."

"Worry me?" Jeannie gave a throaty laugh. "I see you yesterday, you're ripping off old Charlie's head."

Dana winced. The pizza trembled in her stomach.

"Then, next thing I hear, you've been canned."

"That isn't entirely accurate."

"McKenna didn't fire you?"

Dana slicked the tip of her tongue along her bottom lip. "In a way."

"You got fired, but only in a way?"

"I quit."

"Before or after he fired you?"

"What's the difference?"

"Well, if you want to collect unemployment—"

"For goodness' sake, is that all everybody can think about? Unemployment insurance?"

"Who's everybody?"

Dana waved her hand. "You, Arthur..."

"Well, for once Arthur and I agree. Money's important at a time like this."

"Other things are more important, Jeannie."

"For instance?"

"For instance, what did McKenna say?"

"About what?"

Be careful, Dana... "About—about how I left. I mean, did he say he fired me? Or that I quit?"

"I just told you. The word is that he fired you."

Dana frowned and looked down at her slipper-clad toes. A bit of lint was clinging to one fuzzy sole. She bent and plucked it off.

"And?" she said.

"And, what?"

"And, is that all? McKenna didn't say...anything more?"

"McKenna didn't say anything, period. Not to me, anyway. You forget, I am female. I am not one of the chosen few who carries the wondrous Y chromosome. I do not get to sit at his feet and hear him pontificate. What I'm telling you is only what I heard via the ever-trusty grapevine."

"Oh."

"Oh, indeed. Why? Is there something more to the story?"

"No," Dana said quickly, "of course not."

"You sure?" Jeannie's voice lowered dramatically. "Tell me what he did, Dana. You can trust me."

"He didn't do anything. I don't know what you mean."

"Oh, come on. Did he do something totally outrageous?"

Dana flushed. "Of course not."

"Something you still can't believe?"

"No! Why would you ever think—"

"He made a pass," Jeannie said with delight.

"He did not!" It wasn't a lie. What McKenna had done had nothing to do with sex and everything to do with power.

"Oh," Jeannie sounded disappointed. "Well, what then?"

"I just told you, he didn't do anything."

"Did he lose his cool?"

Dana closed her eyes. Had Griffin lost his cool? She'd thought so, just for a minute or two, when he'd been kissing her that second time, when he'd made that soft, growling sound and drawn her close.

But he hadn't. It had all been an act; he'd proved that when he'd put her from him and given her that arrogant, I'm-such-a-stud smile.

"No," she said, her tone an icy match for the memory of that smile. "He did not lose his cool. He told me he was letting me go, so I said I was quitting, and then he told me to collect my paycheck and never to darken Data Bytes's doorstep again." She sighed and sank down on the sofa. "Or words to that effect."

"Wow."

"Wow, indeed. Now, I have to look for another job and worry about what kind of reference I'm going to get from Data Bytes."

"Yeah," Jeannie said. "Well, that explains a lot."

"What does?"

"That he gave you the old heave-ho. And that old Dave, so they say, got el stinko."

Dana's eyes widened. "Really?"

"That's the rumor."

"Did McKenna know?"

"He must have. Word is, he went ballistic."

"What do you mean? What happened?"

"Well, today's the start of the big Miami Beach conference, remember?"

Dana sighed. "How could I forget?"

"Dave's supposed to show everybody how the new program shines."

"He couldn't have. The code is a mess."

"Uh-huh. And the word is that McKenna finally knows it."

"Don't count on it. I tried and tried to warn him—"

"I saw him at the keyboard, myself."

"Are you serious? What keyboard?"

"At the computer. Dave's first, and then yours. He sat there, tap-tap-tapping away—"

Dana's doorbell rang. She frowned and glanced at her watch. It was almost seven-thirty. Who could be calling at such an hour?

"—Doing everything he could to get the code to work, but it was a no-go."

"Hang on, Jeannie. There's someone at the door."

"At seven-something in the morning? Be careful, okay? I don't think Jack the Ripper rings the doorbell when he comes calling, but you can never tell."

Dana smiled. "It's probably José," she said as she rose to her feet.

Jeannie giggled. "Dana, you devil. And all the time, I thought good old Arthur was the only guy who held the key to your heart."

"José's my paper boy. He usually collects on Saturday morning, but sometimes..."

The bell rang again. José was certainly impatient today.

"So," Dana said as she tucked the phone between her ear and her shoulder and undid all the locks but the final chain, "tell me more about McKenna."

"What's to tell? You know everything I do. There he was at quitting time, staring first at Dave's monitor and then at yours, doing a fast two-finger shuffle on the keys, cursing and muttering and slugging down cup after cup of coffee while he tried to coax the code's secrets from the system."

Dana snorted. "Griffin McKenna," she said as she opened the door, "could probably get a hundred women into his bed faster than he could get that code from the comp... Oh, my God!"

"Dana?" Jeannie said. "Dana? What is it? Listen, I was only joking about Jack the Ripper..."

Dana stared through the door opening. Jack the Ripper would have been easier to accept than reality.

"You're wrong," Griffin McKenna said tonelessly. "I could get a thousand women into my bed faster than I can get that damned code out of that computer."

"Dana?" Jeannie's voice was frantic. "Who's there? Talk to me!"

"Open the door, Anderson."

Maybe he wasn't real. Maybe he was an apparition.

"I assure you," Griffin said coldly, "this is strictly business."

"Dana? Dana, say something!"

"Open the door. And you'd better say something, to silence that hysterical female on the other end of the line."

He was real, all right. And really furious. She could see it in the way he stood before her, arms folded, eyes and mouth narrowed.

"Miz Anderson?"

Dana looked past Griffin's shoulder. José looked back at her.

"You okay, Miz Anderson?"

Griffin glanced over his shoulder. "She's fine," he said. His gaze locked on Dana's. "Aren't you, Anderson?"

She looked from the man to the boy. Then, wordlessly, she undid the chain, took the newspaper from José's hands and let Griffin brush past her into the living room.

"Dana," Jeannie screeched, "talk to me!"

Griffin folded his arms over his chest. "Talk to her," he said. He looked at José. "And to your would-be rescuer."

Dana swallowed. Could she talk? Her lips felt numb. "Everything's fine," she said to José and to Jeannie. "Honestly."

José nodded and headed for the stairs. Jeannie was more persistent.

"Somebody's there," she said. "Right?"

"Yes. And I've got to go now."

"You want me to call nine-one-one?"

Dana felt an insane desire to laugh. "Nine-one-one can't help me."

"No one can," McKenna said. His smile was chill. "Except for me."

"Dana?"

Dana licked her lips. "I'm fine, Jeannie."

"Really?"

"Really."

"Call me later, okay?"

Dana nodded. She took the phone from her ear, pressed the off button, and looked Griffin straight in the eye.

"You have two minutes to explain why you're here," she said. "And then—"

"And then," he said with a chilly smile, "you'll call nine-one-one?"

She dumped the phone and the newspaper on the table. Then she took a step back, feet apart, hands slightly lifted, palms angled out, and told herself there was no way McKenna could hear the thump-thump of her heart.

"And then," she said, "so help me Hannah, I'll give you a kick where it'll do the most good. And I promise you, McKenna, you won't be doing any boasting about how many women you can get into your bed after that. Not for a very, very long time."

CHAPTER FIVE

IF IT was true that looks could kill, Griffin figured he'd have been lying at Dana's feet, breathing his last by now.

There was no mistaking the message in her eyes. If he clutched at his throat, gasped, and fell to the floor, the only thing she'd do would be applaud.

A muscle twitched in his jaw.

Her threat to kick him should have been a laugh, considering her size compared to his, but that steely-eyed expression couldn't be ignored. There were times that guts could make up for lack of expertise. He'd learned that the first few months he'd spent swimming in the shark-infested waters of Wall Street, and he'd learned it well.

On the other hand, she didn't hold a monopoly on anger. His was every bit as hot as hers. Hotter, maybe, considering that he'd spent most of the night slaving over a computer that might as well have been the Sphinx, considering its smug refusal to give up its secrets.

Griffin eyed Dana. She was still standing poised like a female martial arts expert, feet apart, arms outstretched, hands ready to chop him into tiny pieces.

She had no idea how easily he could get past that fancy stance of hers. Griffin almost smiled. He worked out a few hours a week at a gym used by amateur boxers. It was a place that smelled of sweat and liniment instead of cologne and air freshener. A long time ago, back in his college days, he'd learned that a guy could get a pretty good workout punching the big body bag, develop quick hands on the speed bag, and get all the aerobics he needed, skipping rope.

That was what he did now, a couple of times a week. His footwork wasn't fancy, but it was quick, and so were his jabs—quick enough so that one move would take him right inside her blocking defense. Then, using nothing but his size and weight, he'd have her where he wanted her, right down on the floor.

Down on the floor, with him on top of her.

Dammit, what was wrong with him? He did not like the Anderson woman. Never had, never would. She wasn't his type. Come to think of it, she wouldn't be any man's type, not the way she looked this morning. The prim and proper Ms. Anderson of the office had given way to an entirely different woman. Her hair was loose. It looked damp, as if she'd just showered, and it was drying in soft-looking curls. She was wearing a sweatshirt , faded jeans and a pair of slippers that had definitely seen better days. Whose picture was that on the sweatshirt? Griffin frowned.

His brows rose. Damned if it wasn't Lois Lane.

"Lois Lane?" he said without thinking.

"Yes," Dana's chin lifted a notch. "You want to make something out of it, McKenna?"

"No," he said quickly. "No, Lois Lane is..."

Is what? What was he doing? Who cared if it was Lois Lane? She could have Quasimodo on her sweatshirt, for all he cared. What mattered was that she'd screwed up the computer code, or maybe she was the only one who could unscrew it, or—or...

Was she braless? She seemed to be. He could see the high, rounded outline of her breasts move as she breathed. And those jeans. They clung to her like a second skin, outlining her gently rounded hips, accentuating her long legs.

"I know what you're thinking, McKenna."

Griffin's gaze flew to meet Dana's.

"And I wouldn't try it, if I were you. I've got a black belt in karate."

He nodded, knowing damn well that she had no idea what he was thinking because if she did, she'd have come at him like a wildcat.

"Really," he said.

Dana nodded. It wasn't a complete lie. She'd have had a black belt by now, if she'd continued taking classes, but that was none of his business.

"If you don't believe me, just try something."

Griffin thought back to the long night he'd put in. It cooled his passion a lot faster than Anderson's puny threat. How many hours had he spent trying to make that miserable code work?

"Y'll never do it," Forrester had slurred, after Griffin had poured a pot of black coffee down the man's gullet. "That Anderson broad ish one smart cookie."

Griffin had looked up from the keyboard. "I thought you said she was incompetent."

"Yeah, that, too."

"Which is it, Dave? Was she incompetent, or was she smart?"

"She's smart enough to have screwed up the program, thass for sure."

Forrester had guffawed at his own wit, hiccuped loudly, curled up in the corner and fallen into the sleep of the dead. Disgusted, Griffin had left him there. At four, he'd given up trying to make the code work. Instead, he'd typed a letter informing Forrester that he was lucky he was only being fired, stapled it to the jerk's lapel, and then he'd headed home to shower and catch a couple of hours' shut-eye, after which he'd finally acknowledged that there was only one possible hope of saving Data Bytes—which was why he told himself, now, to calm down and remember that more flies had been caught with honey than with vinegar.

"You hear me, McKenna?" Dana narrowed her eyes. "Give me the slightest cause, and I'll give you a very bad time."

Griffin fixed a solemn expression on his face.

"I'm sure you could," he said, lying without a blink.

Dana nodded. "Damn right."

"But there's no need to take this hard-line approach with me."

She snorted in derision. "There's every need. Did you think I'd forgotten what you did?"

She meant the kiss. He knew that, but swimming with the sharks had also taught him that there were times it paid to play dumb.

"No," he said, "of course not. How could I have forgotten such a memorable moment?" A delicate wash of pink flowed up under her skin. Good, he thought grimly. Let her suffer a little. She could use the practice. He dragged out the seconds as long as he could, before dropping the other shoe. "I assure you, I never forget the sad moment when I'm forced to fire a valued employee."

Her face was a study in total bewilderment.

"Fired?" she said. "But I thought—I thought you were referring to—to—"

"Referring to what?" he said politely.

The color in her cheeks went from pink to rose. At last, she cleared her throat, straightened her posture, and folded her arms over her chest.

"What are you doing here, McKenna? Explain, and make it snappy."

Touchy broad, Griffin thought, and smiled through his teeth.

"Do you think we could have some privacy, while I explain?" he said, jerking his chin toward the open door.

Dana didn't take her eyes off him.

"No."

"You like having an audience?" Griffin smiled again "Hey, that's fine with me."

Dana looked past him. Mrs. Gibbs, who lived across the hall, was standing in the open doorway to her apartment. She was wearing a pink robe, a headful of curlers, and a rapt expression that meant she already had enough gossip to last a week, down in the basement laundry room.

"Hello, dearie," Mrs. Gibbs said. "Who's your handsome visitor?"

"He isn't—"

"He certainly is." Mrs. Gibbs batted her lashes in Griffin's direction. "Hello."

"Hello."

"Ooh, look at that smile! Aren't you going to introduce us, dearie?"

Dana rolled her eyes. "Oh, for God's sake..."

"I'm Griffin McKenna," Griffin said pleasantly.

"Her boyfriend?"

"Her boss. Well, her former boss. Ms. Anderson is no longer—"

Dana slammed the door shut and glared at him. "Why not rent a billboard?"

"Sorry. I didn't know your termination was to be kept a secret."

"I quit, remember?"

"A matter of semantics, Anderson."

"A matter of fact, McKenna. You have one minute to explain what you're doing here."

"That's fifty seconds more than I'll need."

"Good. Because when the minute is up—"

"What in hell did you do to my code?"

Dana's eyes widened. "I beg your pardon?"

"I said—"

"I heard what you said, McKenna. Are you crazy? I didn't do anything to your code."

"Forrester says—"

"Besides, that code isn't yours."

"Really," Griffin smiled tightly. "And who, pray tell, owns Data Bytes?"

"You may have enough money to make you think you can buy the world, McKenna, but you don't have the brains to—"

He moved fast, so fast that she knew instinctively she'd been lucky to get away with the karate bit only moments ago. His hands clamped down on her forearms, not hard enough to hurt but hard enough to lift her to her toes.

"You've got brass, Anderson." His blue gaze bored into her. "Anybody ever tell you that?"

Dana's heart thudded. She could see a little muscle jumping just beside his mouth. That handsome mouth, that had been so warm, so hot, on hers.

"Let me go, McKenna."

"Why?" His voice was low and just a little rough. "A little while ago, you were busy making it clear you weren't afraid of me."

"I'm not."

His hands slid up and clasped her shoulders. His gaze dropped to her mouth. She could feel the weight of that gaze, the heat of it, as surely as if he were stroking her mouth with the tip of his finger. As surely as if he were putting his lips against hers.

"I think you are," he said softly.

She pulled away from him and stepped back. This was a game for him, that was what it was. She knew that, and yet she was playing right into it.

"What I meant," she said briskly, "is that owning a software company doesn't necessarily make you capable of understanding computer code."

"And what *I* meant," Griffin said just as briskly, "is that the code was developed by Dave Forrester, who worked for me." His smile was pure arrogance. "And that makes the code mine."

Dana stepped around him, snatching her coffee cup from the table as she made her way to the kitchen.

"Fine. Believe what you want. It doesn't mean a damn to me, anymore."

"Forrester says you screwed up."

"So you said when you terminated me." Dana dumped the remnants of her cold coffee into the sink and poured a fresh cup. "I repeat, believe what you want."

Griffin frowned, looked at the coffee that remained in the pot and then at Dana.

"Who makes the coffee that was in that mug in your office?"

Dana blinked. "What?"

"There's a big yellow mug on the desk in your office. There was some cold stuff in it that was oily and black and smelled like it might have been coffee, in a former lifetime. Who made it? You?"

"No. SueEllen did. She works down the hall in—"

"In that case," Griffin said, nodding toward the coffeepot, "I'll take a cup of that stuff."

"I beg your pardon?"

"I said—"

"I heard what you said, McKenna. What I didn't hear was me offering you some."

Griffin shook his head, reached past her, took a cup from the shelf and filled it.

"Your hospitality leaves something to be desired, Anderson," He took a long swallow from the cup. "This is much better."

Dana rolled her eyes. "What are you, McKenna? A financial genius or a coffee connoisseur?"

"A survivor." The corners of his mouth twitched. "I couldn't decide if that coffee in your office was an experiment gone bad or a secret formula for motor oil."

Dana laughed. She hadn't meant to, but when she thought of all the times she'd shuddered and glugged down SueEllen's guaranteed-to-keep-your-eyeballs-popping coffee as she worked late into the night, the laugh just came bubbling up.

Griffin laughed, too. Her pulse rate danced. He was incredibly handsome when he laughed. Well, he was always handsome, but when he laughed—when he laughed, he was...

The telephone rang. Dana swung toward it, closed her eyes for a second, then picked it up.

"Dana."

"Arthur." Good old Arthur. Dear Arthur. Arthur, her ever-reliable anchor to reality. The feeling of relief was so intense that she almost felt giddy. "Oh, I'm so glad to hear your voice."

"And I'm glad to hear yours. Are you feeling better now?"

"Better?"

"You were so upset last night, that I wondered—"

"Anderson?" Griffin said.

Dana frowned. "I'm sorry, Arthur. I missed that. What did you say?"

"I haven't got all day, Anderson. Tell whoever that is that you're busy."

Dana clapped her hand over the mouthpiece. "I am no longer your employee, McKenna. I don't have to take orders from you."

"As if you ever did."

"Dana?" Arthur said. "Is somebody there?"

Dana sighed and put the phone to her ear again.

"Yes, Arthur. Griffin McKenna is here."

"There? In your apartment?"

She sighed again. Arthur sounded as if she'd just told him the President had stepped out of the woodwork.

"That's right."

"Why is he there, Dana?"

"I don't know, Arthur. He hasn't deigned to tell me, yet."

Griffin frowned. "Is that the Bow Tie?"

Dana made a face.

"He hasn't tried anything unseemly, Dana, has he?"

"No. It's nothing like that, Arthur."

"I'll bet he's there because he's concerned you'll go to the unemployment people and demand a hearing."

"What's he saying?" Griffin demanded, and moved closer.

Dana turned her back. "You're probably right."

"Excellent news, my dear, excellent. Perhaps you'd like to let me speak with Mr. McKenna."

"No. No, Arthur, that isn't necessary."

"What's the problem?" Griffin leaned over her shoulder, his breath warm against her temple. "Is he afraid I'm poaching?"

"Well, then, Dana, let me give you some quick advice. Remember that your rights are governed by law—"

"Did you tell him that you kissed me?" he whispered.

Dana swung around and glared at him. "I did not!"

"Did not what?" Arthur said. "Dana, no matter what the man tries to tell you, your rights are—"

"I'll call you back, Arthur," She slammed down the phone and looked up at Griffin. "You said you'd tell me why you came here, McKenna. Well, I'm waiting."

Griffin frowned. Why *had* he come here? He couldn't remember. The scent of Dana's hair was in his nostrils. He'd reminded her of that kiss just to annoy her and the Bow Tie, but that had turned out to be a mistake. The kiss was all he could think of now, the feel of her mouth, the little sound she'd made when he'd parted her lips with his...

He took a step back, and cleared his throat.

"I came here to ask about the code, Anderson."

"What about it?"

"Is Forrester right? Did you screw it up?"

"How many ways do you want me to say 'no,' McKenna? Now, if that's all—"

"It isn't."

Dana blew a curl from her forehead. "Make it quick, okay? I have things to do this morning."

"Like, looking for a new job," Griffin said with a tight smile.

"Get to it, McKenna. What do you want?"

"How big a part did you play in the development of the code?"

She opened her mouth, prepared to give him a snide response, but something in the way he was looking at her stopped her.

"A major part," she said.

"Fifty-fifty, with Forrester?"

She smiled coldly. "He only wishes."

"Let's put it this way, Anderson. Can you debug that code and make the program run the way it should?"

"You mean, rather than debate whether or not I developed it, you'll settle for knowing if I can fix it?"

"That's one way of putting it, I suppose."

Dana banged down her coffee cup. "You are the most chauvinistic, insolent, impossible man I've ever known!"

"Thank you," Griffin said politely. "But I didn't come here to be complimented."

"Oh, for heaven's sake—"

Griffin caught her arm as she started past him.

"I haven't finished delivering my message, Anderson." He looked up at her kitchen clock. "The Data Bytes rep has to be in Florida by one this afternoon."

"How nice," Dana said with a glittering smile. "He'll be just in time for lunch."

"There are meetings scheduled from one-thirty until five this evening, and there's a dinner tonight with—"

"He'll be a busy little bee, won't he?" she said brightly.

"If this weekend's a fiasco, Data Bytes will probably collapse."

She sighed and fluttered her lashes. "And you'll lose money. But I'm sure you aren't thinking of that, not one little bit."

"A lot of people will lose their jobs. Can you make jokes about that, too, Anderson?"

She looked at him, her eyes gone cold. "You're right, they will. I tried to warn you, McKenna."

"So you did."

"Yes. So I did. And now you're in trouble."

"The company is in trouble."

"Forgive me for asking, but is there a difference?"

Griffin put down his coffee cup. "Ask the people who stand to lose their jobs that question. See what they say."

He had her there. It was true, as Data Bytes went, so went McKenna...but so went Jeannie, and Charlie the Custodian, and SueEllen, and a couple of hundred others.

"You're right," she said after a minute.

"I know I am, and believe me, it gives me no pleasure."

"I should hope it doesn't! If you'd only listened to the truth—"

"Meaning, I should have listened when you told me about

Forrester." He nodded. "Yes. I should have." Griffin jammed his hands into his pockets. "I shouldn't have fired you, either."

Dana shrugged. She couldn't gloat, not with all the jobs in the balance.

"It really wouldn't have made any difference. I could never have gotten the program up and running by this morning."

"Neither could Forrester."

"If he'd had a little more time, if he'd have been running on all cylinders, maybe..." She smiled ruefully. "My mother used to say that if 'if' ruled the world, nobody would worry about getting to heaven."

Griffin smiled. "The lady was a philosopher."

"A pragmatist," Dana said with no smile at all. "All right, McKenna. Apology accepted. Now, if you don't mind—"

"What were you going to say? About what would have happened, if Forrester were functional?"

Dana tucked a loose strand of hair behind her ear. She moved past Griffin, into the living room, and sat down on the sofa. She put her feet up on the planked coffee table and crossed them.

"Anderson?"

She looked up. Griffin had seated himself opposite her, in the wooden rocker she'd salvaged from a pile of trash at the curb. It was old and beat-up looking, but it seemed to have taken on a certain elegance, thanks to its occupant.

"You were saying, about Forrester?"

Dana cleared her throat. "I was just saying that if he were sober, there was a chance—a slim one, you understand—that he just might have gotten you through the weekend."

"Get me through, how?"

Amazing. When Arthur sat in the rocker, it was just an ordinary, slightly beat-up chair, but Griffin—Griffin gave it a very different look. Had the chair always been this small? Or was it just that he was so big?

"Anderson?"

Dana blinked.

"How do you mean, he might have gotten me through the weekend?"

"Well, even though he didn't really develop the code, he did work with me. And he's really a genius—when he's sober, anyway. So, he could probably have made the code behave. Not completely, of course, but with a little luck, he might have at least gotten the demos to work." She sighed and put her feet down on the floor, side by side. "But he can't, so what's the point of talking about it?"

Griffin looked at her for a long minute. Then he sat back, folded his arms and began, gently, to move the rocker back and forth.

"So, what you're saying is that you developed the code..."

"For the most part."

"...But only Forrester could have made it work this weekend."

Dana's head snapped up. "I never said that!"

"You did. You just finished telling me that—"

"I said, Forrester—a sober Forrester—might have pulled it off because Forrester is your employee."

"Ah. I see. Someone else could manage, then."

"Not really. Not unless that person had a couple of days to get up to speed on the ins and outs of the program."

"But, if that were possible?"

Dana lifted one shoulder. "A guy who's good, who understands the nuances of the code...a guy like that might be able to get you through the weekend."

"'A guy,'" Griffin said, and smiled.

Dana rose from the sofa. "A figure of speech, McKenna. A 'he,' a 'she,' an 'it.' I'm referring to a hypothetical person who's a computer whiz. A person with ability, training, talent and—"

"And knowledge."

"Exactly. And a sober Dave Forrester is the only person at Data Bytes who fits that bill."

"There's only one problem with that reasoning, Anderson." Griffin's eyes met hers. "Forrester isn't with Data Bytes anymore. I fired that miserable drunk this morning." He smiled, and Dana thought she knew how a caged canary would feel under the steady gaze of a sleek cat. "No one at Data Bytes fits that bill," he said softly. "But you do."

Dana shot to her feet. Was that what this was all about? Did McKenna think she'd go back to working for him? Did he think he could talk her into taking on a job that was damn near impossible? After he'd fired her, swallowed all of Forrester's damnable lies, accused her of everything from incompetency to sabotage?

"Forget it," she snapped.

Griffin rose, too, his gaze locked on hers.

"I already apologized, Anderson. What more can I do?"

"You're breaking my heart," Dana said coldly.

"It's not your heart I'm aiming for, it's your brain. Think about all those innocent people who'll suffer, just because of your hurt feelings."

"Is that what you think? That you wounded my ego?" She glared at him. "I've got a message for you, McKenna—"

"If I introduce that program in Florida this weekend, it'll be the end of the company, and you know it."

"Oh, that's great! But it won't work. You can't lay this off on me, mister!"

"Dammit, are you dense? You're the one who has the best chance of getting us through this."

"Us? *Us?* There is no 'us,' remember? I am not a Data Bytes employee anymore."

"But you could be. And, if you were, you'd have the best shot anybody could have of pulling us out of this mess."

"The best shot at saving your ass, McKenna, isn't that what you mean?"

"My, my, Anderson, how you do talk!"

"Spit it out, McKenna. What do you want from me?"

His grin was charming, almost boyish, but there was no mistaking the flat determination in his eyes.

"If Data Bytes goes under, everybody drowns."

"We agree on something, anyway. So?"

"So, come back on board."

Dana stared at Griffin. He was begging now... The hell he was. He was looking at her as if *he* were doing *her* a favor, as if he'd expected her to leap for joy, throw her arms around his neck...

"No," she said firmly, looking straight into his eyes.

"No?" he said, looking stunned.

"That's right. No. I don't want my job back, and that's final."

A smile tugged at his mouth. "Ah, but I didn't offer you your job back, now, did I?"

Color flew into Dana's face. Damn the man! She'd let him make a fool of her again.

"Get out, McKenna," she said, stalking past him. "Just turn around, walk to the door, and—"

"What I'm offering you is a new position."

She stopped dead. "A new position?"

"Certainly. You'll take Forrester's spot."

She turned, very slowly, half expecting him to laugh, but his expression was solemn.

"Forrester's spot?"

"Of course."

Dana nodded, as if she'd understood that all along.

"I'd expect a raise in pay," she said calmly.

"I've already told as much to Payroll."

"You've already..." She rolled her eyes. "Has anyone ever told you what an arrogant so-and-so you are, McKenna?"

"Many. And, before you get your feathers ruffled, I also told Payroll you'd be getting a forty percent pay raise."

"Oh, really," she said, her words dripping with sarcasm. "And I suppose you think that a—that a..." Dana's eyes widened. "Did you say, forty percent?"

"Not enough?" He smiled, but without humor. "Fifty, then."

Dana put her hands behind her back and crossed all her fingers. "I want a contract with stock options. And the executive medical plan."

He nodded. "Done."

"New furniture, in Forrester's office." She smiled coolly. "I'm not much for metal desks and old file cabinets stuffed with back issues of a girlie magazine."

"Pick whatever you like." He held out his hand. "Is it a deal?"

Dana looked at his hand, then at him. "Not quite."

To her surprise, he laughed. "Okay, get your pound of flesh while you can. What else do you want? A secretary of your own? Done. A staff to do the drudge work? Fine. Come on, Anderson. What more can there possibly be?"

"A title. Vice president in charge of research sounds just fine," she said, and waited, because even she knew that now she had pushed him too far.

"If you were a man," Griffin said softly, "I'd say you had...guts." His gaze moved over her with excruciating slowness. "But if there's one thing you most definitely are not, it's male."

Color flooded her cheeks again, but she held herself stiffly. "Is it a deal, or isn't it?"

"You are some piece of work, Anderson."

"I'm a piece of work you need, McKenna."

He nodded. "All right. You're the new V.P. of Research and Development. How's that sound?"

How did it sound? Like a miracle. Could she answer his question without letting him know that her heart was racing like an out-of-control train?

"It sounds fine," she said with what she hoped was admirable restraint.

"Everthing's contingent on you getting Data Bytes through this weekend, of course."

Dana nodded. "Of course."

"Let's shake on it, then."

He held out his hand again. She looked at it. Then, slowly, she put her hand in his.

Their fingers touched. Clung. She felt the heat of his skin. His fingers tightened around hers...

Dana snatched back her hand. "It's—it's getting late."

Griffin frowned, shot back his cuff again, and his frown became a scowl. "Bloody hell! Can you pack in twenty minutes?"

She laughed, and tried not to sound as giddy as she felt. "Time me."

He looked at her. Her face was flushed, her eyes were as bright as stars, and he had to fight back the overwhelming urge to take her into his arms and kiss her until that look of joy, of sheer delight, was for him and not for a job.

He stepped back.

"Get to it, then," he said gruffly. "My car's waiting downstairs."

She turned on her heel and fled into the bedroom. The door slammed shut. He could hear the sounds of drawers opening and closing. Less than ten minutes later she reappeared, dressed in a tailored shirt, a tailored skirt, and low-heeled, sensible shoes, carrying a small carry-on suitcase and her portable computer.

Griffin nodded in approval.

"Eight minutes, Anderson, and here you are, dressed for success, as usual, and all packed. And I see you've even managed to find time to clamp your hair to your head."

There was something in his tone. Dana frowned and touched her hand to the neat knot at the back of her head. "Is there something wrong with it?"

"No," he said, his face virtually expressionless. "It looks just the way it always does."

"Well, then." She smiled. "I told you I'd be ready in time, McKenna."

Griffin reached for her carry-on. They wrestled over it for a couple of seconds before she gave up fighting and let him take it.

They rode the elevator to the lobby in silence. It had started snowing sometime during the early morning hours; the city streets seemed strangely hushed and almost pristine. Griffin put his hand lightly on Dana's elbow and led her to the

Mercedes at the curb. His driver opened the door and she stepped inside.

"La Guardia Airport, please, Oliver," Griffin said as he sat down beside her. "And see what you can do to get us there as quickly as possible."

They were almost at the terminal when Dana turned toward him.

"I'll be in touch, of course."

"In touch?"

"Yes. I'll call you from Miami and keep you updated on the situation."

Griffin thought of telling her that she wouldn't have to do that, but just then Oliver pulled the car to the curb.

"I want you to know that I won't fail you, Mr. McKenna," Dana said as she scooted toward the door. "I'm not promising anything, you understand, I simply mean that I'll do my best to get Data Bytes through the weekend."

"I hope you succeed, for all our sakes."

Oliver opened the door. Dana, then Griffin, stepped onto the sidewalk. "There's no need to walk me inside, Mr. McKenna."

"What's going on here, Anderson? You've taken to addressing me as Mr. McKenna again."

"Well, it's the polite thing to do. After all, I work for you now." She smiled as she reached for her carry-on. "If things don't work out and you fire me again, I'll undoubtedly call you by other names. Goodbye, Mr. McKenna," she said very politely, and held out her hand.

Griffin took her hand in his. "Hello, Ms. Anderson," he said just as politely.

Dana frowned. "I don't understand."

"It's simple." He took his suitcase from Oliver, clasped Dana's elbow firmly, and turned her toward the terminal, knowing, even as he did, that he was probably about to hear some of those names. "You and I are going to Miami together."

CHAPTER SIX

GRIFFIN could almost see the lightbulb go on over Dana's head.

She stopped, processed his statement, then swung around to face him.

"What did you just say?"

Amazing, he thought, how very calm she sounded. Ominously calm. He wasn't fooled, not for a second. He had seen that look in her eye only a little while before. He had the feeling she was seconds away from her karate imitation.

"You heard me," he said, and took her arm. "I'm going to this conference with you."

"You are not!"

"Keep walking, please, Ms. Anderson. We're late."

"We're going to be even later, unless you tell me you're joking."

"Do I sound as if I'm joking?"

Dana looked up at Griffin as he hurried her through the terminal. He most definitely did not look as if he were joking, she thought, and her stomach took a tumble.

"Get this through your head, McKenna. You have as about as much chance of going with me as—as a pig has of flying!"

"A fascinating image, Anderson."

"*Will* you let go of my arm?" she said furiously. "I do not wish to be dragged through this terminal like a package."

"And I don't intend to stand here and debate an issue that's not on my agenda. We're running late. How many times to I have to say it?"

"What's with this *we* stuff? I am going to Florida. You are not going with me."

They had reached the security checkpoint. Griffin dumped their luggage on the counter.

"Put your computer on the belt, Anderson."

"Like hell I will!"

"Oh, for... Put the damned thing down," he growled, peeling the case from her grasp. None too gently, he put his hand in the small of her back, propelled her through the security gate and followed after. "*I* am going to Miami," he said, snatching up all the luggage as it emerged from the X-ray machine. "And *you* are going with me."

"I am not! And I can carry my own stuff."

"I'm sure that's true," he said, ignoring her efforts to wrestle her things from his grasp. "You can do anything a man can do, only a hundred times better,"

"You've got that right."

"Gate seven," Griffin said, nudging her to the left. "That's us."

"There is no 'us,' McKenna."

"A figure of speech, I assure you." Griffin shot her a cold smile. "A man would have to have a death wish, to want a woman like you in his life."

"Believe me, the feeling is mutual." Dana glared at him. "Will you slow down?"

"If I do, we'll miss our plane. I keep telling you, we're late."

"And I keep telling *you*, it isn't *our* plane. It's my plane. And it isn't even board—"

"Attention, please. Passengers for East Coast Air, Flight 356 to Miami. Your flight is now boarding at Gate Seven."

Dana grabbed Griffin's arm and swung out in front of him.

"You lied to me," she said. "You told me the Data Bytes rep had to be in Miami by one this afternoon!"

"And he will be, if you'll just shut up and keep moving."

"You don't know a damn thing about computers. You admitted that yourself."

"Precisely."

"So what's the point in you being there?"

He laughed. "I hate to point this out to you, Anderson, but I own the company."

"And *I* hate to point this out to *you*, but that isn't going to impress those people one iota."

Griffin shot her a smug grin. "It will, when they realize we've got a great new program."

"You hope," Dana muttered.

"These are business people who'll be at that conference, Anderson. As far as they're concerned, I *am* Data Bytes!"

"My god, you are unbelievable! A walking ego, is what you are."

"Going face-to-face with the guy at the top gives people a feeling of confidence."

"Humph."

"Trust me, Anderson. It's the truth. It's how I got where I am today."

"You got there by being born with a silver spoon in your mouth."

Griffin swung her toward him. "I got there by working my tail off," he said coldly. "The same as you."

"Oh, spare me, McKenna. You were born rich. Everything's come easy to you, while people like me..."

"While people like you, what?"

Dana shook her head. "Nothing. You wouldn't understand."

"You're a snob, lady. Anybody ever tell you that? You think that anybody who was born to money is useless."

"That isn't true!"

"It damn well is." His mouth twisted. "Well, let me tell you something. Not that it's any of your damn business, but I worked my way through college, the same as you."

"That's ridic..." Dana's eyes narrowed. "How do you know I worked my way through college?"

"I checked your personnel file, that's how." Griffin began hurrying her toward their departure gate. "Did you really think I'd offer you a vice presidency without making sure you had the stuff to warrant it?"

"You didn't offer me the vice presidency. I demanded..."
She looked at him and saw that same opinionated little smile
on his lips again. "Dammit, McKenna! You came prepared to
give me this job, didn't you?"

"Let's just say I came prepared, period. Good planning's at
the heart of success. That's how come I know you went to
Harvard, made the Dean's List, all eight semesters, made Phi
Bete..." He grinned. "An impressive record, Anderson.
Almost as impressive as mine."

"I'll bet."

Griffin laughed. "Well, first I got tossed out of two different
schools, but once I had to pay my own way, I settled down
and... Ah. Here we are. Gate Seven." He dropped the luggage
and dug in his pocket for their boarding passes. "Got 'em.
Let's go."

His story—his half-told story, undoubtedly invented for her,
right on the spot—had taken Dana's mind off the present situation. Now, as he nodded at the boarding gate, she came to
her senses.

"No way." She took a step back. "I am not going anywhere
with you, McKenna."

"I see I don't rate being addressed quite so formally anymore."

"Damn right, you don't. Debug the code by yourself, pal.
I'm not going."

"Don't be an idiot!"

"You've got that right. That's why I'm not—"

"Okay, let's cut to the chase." Griffin looked straight at
ner, his expression cool. "Are you going to be my new V.P.—
or are you going to play it coy?"

"Coy?" Dana said angrily, glaring up at that stony face
with its firmly set mouth and cold eyes. "What's that supposed
to mean?"

"It means I know why you won't go with me."

"I hope you do, McKenna! I just hope you understand how
insulting it is, that you have so little faith in me that you think
you have to go along and ride herd."

Griffin smiled. It was the kind of self-confident smile that made Dana want to wipe it off his face.

"You're scared," he said very softly.

"Me?" Dana snorted. "Don't be ridiculous! I'm not afraid of anything."

"No?"

"No. I just don't like liars."

His eyes narrowed. "I'm a lot of things, Anderson, but I am *not* a liar."

"You lied about going with me on this trip."

"Why, if I may ask a foolish question, would I have done that?"

Dana hesitated. A faint wash of pink colored her cheeks.

"So you could—so you could—"

"So I could what?"

She swallowed dryly. So you could get me alone someplace, and seduce me, she'd almost said, and wouldn't that have been stupid? Seduce her? Why on earth would he want to do that? She wasn't his type, and that was definitely a relief because *he* was surely not hers. So what if he'd kissed her once? Well, twice, but that first kiss hadn't really counted. It had been a meaningless brush of the lips, nothing like that second kiss, the one that had made her knees buckle.

And that only proved what a master he was at the game.

He was an arrogant male chauvinist to the bone. He was everything women had fought against for generations in a battle still not won—and yet, she knew that there were females of the species who'd want him. Lots of them. Legions, probably, once they got to Miami. The bikini brigade would keep him busy from the time the plane touched down until the second it left.

"So I could what?" Griffin said.

His smile had turned even softer and more knowing; his deep blue eyes were fastened on her face. Her heartbeat stumbled. She'd adopted a cat once, when she was a little girl. Not for long, of course; her stepfather hadn't liked animals. But she could still recall the pleasure of that brief time when the creature had been hers to enjoy. Its sleek beauty, its velvet touch—and the brilliance of its gaze as it watched the drab little sparrows that had scratched in the tiny patch of dirt her mother had called a yard.

A shudder ran through her. Oh, yes, the cat had been a creature of incredible beauty, but once she'd stumbled across it, stalking one of the sparrows, not out of hunger but out of whatever fierce joy it found in the hunt...

She jumped as Griffin reached out and put one finger lightly against her mouth, tracing the fullness of her bottom lip.

"You're afraid," he said, his eyes glittering. "Afraid of what might happen if we spend the weekend alone together."

Dana didn't think, she acted. She dropped her computer, rose up on her toes, dug her hands deep into Griffin's hair and dragged his mouth down to hers.

"Hey," he said, but whatever else he might have been about to say was lost against her mouth as she kissed him, hard.

What was good for the goose was good for the gander, she thought calmly. McKenna had kissed her to prove a point. Well, she could do the same thing...

Maybe not.

A jolt of electricity seemed to arc from his mouth to hers. Her blood sizzled. Oh, she thought, oh...

She pulled back, heart racing. Griffin had the stunned look of a man who's just discovered that the ripsaw he'd been carelessly tinkering with was plugged in all along and could have sliced him into sushi at will.

"Anderson?" he croaked.

Say something, Dana told herself fiercely. For heaven's sake, say something intelligible!

"You see?" Her voice sounded scratchy. She cleared her throat. "You see, Mr. McKenna? If I were afraid of you, fearful I might succumb to your—to whatever, would I have kissed you? Would I be standing here, feeling so cool, calm, and collected?" Stop it, she told her pulse as it gave a hyperactive leap. "No. I would not. So I suggest you get this through your thick skull. I'm not afraid of you, or of spending the weekend in your company." Eyes still locked with his, she reached down and fumbled for the handle of her computer case. "The only thing I'm afraid of is that you'll get underfoot, show your ignorance and keep me from debugging that program."

Griffin opened his mouth, then shut it. For the first time in his life, no words would come.

"Attention, please. This is the final call for Flight 356 to Miami."

Dana snatched her boarding pass from Griffin's hand and brushed past him. "Hurry up, or we'll miss our plane."

A couple of seconds passed. Then Griffin cleared his throat, straightened his tie, picked up his things and followed after her.

What had happened in that terminal?

Griffin sat in the corner of the taxi that was taking them from Miami Airport to the Hotel de las Palmas and tried to figure it out. Hell, he thought uncomfortably, he'd spent the entire flight trying to figure it out. What made him think he'd come up with an answer now?

Cautiously, he shot a quick glance at Dana. She was seated as far from him as she could get, her spine as straight as a board, her knees primly together, her hands folded in her lap. Her profile was serene. For all he knew, she was running code inside her head. That was what she'd done through the whole trip, sat with her computer in her lap and her fingers on the keyboard, angled toward the window in a way that had made it clear she was deliberately excluding him.

His mood took another ten-degree drop. Cool as the proverbial cucumber, he thought grimly. She was the very portrait of a genderless young executive.

No. Not quite.

Griffin's gaze moved over her again. Despite the rigidity of her posture, her skirt had hiked up over her knees, exposing a length of thigh. Her hair was coming out of that tight little knot, too. Soft curls were falling at her temple and against her ear. The last time her hair had come undone, he was the man who'd undone it. He could still remember the silky feel of it in his hands, the sweetness of her mouth as he'd kissed her.

Hell.

He looked away from her and stared blindly out the window.

In the blink of an eye, everything had changed.

That kiss in the office was one thing. But the kiss at the gate... That had been something else.

It wasn't just that she had kissed him, although that had been a shocker all by itself. It was the way she'd done it. So deliberately. So calmly. She'd just grabbed two fistfuls of his hair and hauled his mouth down to hers. He'd been stunned, yeah, but in the first shocked instant, he'd understood.

I'm in control here, she'd been saying.

Except, she hadn't been. And neither had he. In the span of a heartbeat, the kiss had gone from ice to flame. It had almost scalded him—but before he'd had the chance to react, she'd stepped back and fixed him with an unfeeling stare, as if kissing him had been about as exciting as shaking hands with his great-uncle Edgar.

So, which was it? Had she lost control, the same as him? Or was he just plain crazy?

Not that he gave a damn. If the world ran out of women, Dana Anderson would still have to wait her turn until he showed any interest. What intelligent man *would* show interest in a woman like her? She was sharp-tongued and mean-tempered as a shark with a toothache. She hated men; she was obviously sexually repressed and probably terrified of her own femininity.

She was, in other words, one very interesting challenge.

Griffin's scowl grew even darker. Challenge? Ridiculous! Turning Data Bytes around was a challenge. Turning Dana Anderson into a real, live woman was not. Let another man peel away all those outside layers.

The Bow Tie, for example.

But would she ever really let the Bow Tie feel the unexpected heat of that soft mouth? Would he ever know the gut-wrenching frustration of that instant when she fought for control and stumbled back from the edge of the precipice? Could the Bow Tie, or any other man but him, teach her that the fire of passion was far more dangerous than the heat of anger? That a woman could lie in a man's arms without giving up her soul?

Griffin frowned. Dammit, maybe he really was crazy! He leaned forward.

"Driver? Can't this cab go any faster?"

The driver glanced in his mirror and sighed. Another crazy New Yorker, come for the sun but too impatient to slow down and start to relax.

"*Si,*" he said, "no problem," and stepped down harder on the gas.

No problem, was right, Griffin thought. He sat back, folded his arms over his chest, and forced his thoughts to the business that lay ahead.

The Hotel de las Palmas was big, and new, and it was right on the beach.

It looked like an overly decorated wedding cake, awash in pink, cream and several tons of gold leaf.

Dana wouldn't have been surprised if Marilyn Monroe had come slinking down the wide front steps.

"Interesting," Griffin said briskly as they made their way through the ornate lobby.

It was the first word he'd uttered since they'd boarded their plane. Was it a flag of truce? Dana considered, and decided it was. All right, she'd accept the offering. There was no possible way to get through the weekend without a minimum of conversation.

"Very interesting," she said as she matched her steps to his.

Apparently the kiss had done its job. She'd shocked Griffin McKenna into submission. It was a warming thought. A weekend of hard work, making the new program perform, a couple of days spent enduring his company, and it would be over.

They'd head back to New York and, after a couple of weeks, Data Bytes would be secure and he'd move on.

And she—she would be vice president. What a wonderful thing, to happen. Arthur would be so proud. He'd be so—

Dana almost groaned. He'd be so puzzled when he came by this evening to pick her up for dinner and she wasn't there. In all the rush and confusion, she'd never phoned to tell him about any of this.

Well, she'd remedy that the minute she got into her room.

The desk clerk had a pencil-thin mustache and an enormous smile. He wore a dark suit with narrow lapels, accented by a tastefully correct bow tie.

Griffin figured it was one bow tie too many for the week.

Besides, he didn't like the guy's smile. How could a man smile while he said no, there most certainly were no reservations made in the name of the Data Bytes Corporation?

"Check again," Griffin said.

"There is no point, sir. I have searched my data bank. I have no res—"

"Check," Griffin barked.

The clerk was a perpetual smiler, but he wasn't a fool. His fingers raced across the keyboard of his computer terminal.

"I am sorry, sir. We have no record of a reservation for the Data Bytes Corporation."

Griffin glowered at Dana. "Who made the reservations, Anderson?"

"How should I know?"

"That's true," Griffin's tone ripped with sarcasm. "How should you know, indeed? Just because you handled this project—"

So much for the flag of truce. "I didn't handle it. Dave was in charge, remember?"

Griffin frowned and scraped his hand through his hair. "Okay," he said briskly, "Dave probably screwed up and made the reservation in his own name. 'Forrester,'" he told the clerk. "With two r's."

"Forrester, Forrester..." The clerk shook his head. His smile had slipped and become little more than a grimace. "I'm afraid there's nothing here under that name, sir."

"McKenna, then." Griffin tried not to sound as irritable as he felt. It wasn't the clerk's fault the reservations couldn't be found. "Capital M, small c, capital K-e-n-n-a."

"Let me see... I have reservations for a Macintosh, and for a MacDougal, but nothing for McKenna."

Griffin pinched the bridge of his nose between two fingertips.

"I don't suppose it ever occurred to you to follow up on stuff like this, Anderson," he muttered. "Considering that you knew Dave had a problem, I mean."

"Why would it?" She smiled sweetly.

He sighed. When she was right, she was right. "Okay." He looked at the clerk. "So, we have no reservations."

"That is correct, sir."

"Well, we'll just have to remedy that, Mr... " He looked at the man's brass name tag. "Mr. Whitby." Griffin smiled pleasantly. "We'll need a suite."

"Not in this lifetime." Dana's smile was equally pleasant. She turned it on the clerk, who beamed in return. "We'll need two rooms," she said politely. "Two separate rooms, on separate floors."

"We need a corporate suite," Griffin said, ignoring her. "One with a large central parlor, where we can meet with clients, and two bedrooms, *separate* bedrooms, each with a private bath, adjoining the parlor on either side. Do you have such suites, Mr. Whitby?"

Whitby brushed a fleck of lint from his lapel. "Of course, sir."

"Great. That's what we want."

"I'm sure you do, Mr. McKenna." The clerk paused. Griffin could almost hear the drumroll in the background. "Unfortunately, they're gone."

"Gone?"

"The corporate suites went early, I'm afraid. They were booked months ago."

Easy, Griffin told himself. Just take it nice and easy. Reaching across the counter, grabbing the clerk by the ends of his bow tie, wouldn't solve a thing. It was just that that damned smile was getting to him. Hell, the guy would probably keep smiling as he gurgled his last.

"Of course they were," he said soothingly. "In that case, I suppose we'll have to take my assistant's advice. Two rooms, please, Mr. Whitby."

"His vice president's advice," Dana said. "Two rooms, on separate floors. In separate wings, if possible."

"*Three* rooms," Griffin said through his teeth. "On the same floor. Connecting rooms. I assume Housekeeping can remove the bedroom furnishings from the center room and bring in a couch and some chairs, instead?"

"There'd be a fee, of course."

"Of course. But it can be done?"

Whitby sighed. "I'm sure it could, sir—if we had three connecting rooms. But we do not."

Griffin gripped the edge of the counter. "Three adjoining rooms, then."

"I really am sorry, sir."

"Okay, forget about having them adjoin. Just give us three rooms on the same..."

Whitby shook his head. "I don't have three rooms, sir."

"Two rooms, then," Griffin said in a dangerously soft voice.

The clerk's smile was, at long last, beginning to fade. "Sir, I don't have... All the rooms were filled weeks ago."

Griffin's eyes narrowed. "Let me be sure I understand this. You haven't got a reservation in my firm's name, or in my name, or in the name of anybody connected with me. And now you're telling me you haven't got one blasted room available in this entire hotel?"

"I'm afraid that is correct, sir. Well, we do have an accommodation, but—"

"We'll take it."

Dana touched his arm. "McKenna," she whispered.

Griffin swung toward her. "What?"

She looked at the clerk, then at him. "We cannot share a room."

"Did you hear what the man said? This room he's offering us is all there is."

His tone was soft again. Ominously so, but she didn't care.

"I don't care. There is no way I am going to share a room with—"

"Oh, it isn't a room, madam."

Griffin and Dana both looked at the clerk, who swallowed nervously.

"It's a suite."

A slow smile edged across Griffin's face. "A suite?"

"Yes, sir."

Dana cocked her head. "But you just said—"

"He made a mistake," Griffin chuckled. "We all make mistakes, Mr. Whitby, isn't that right?"

"Uh, yes, sir. Well, not exactly, sir. I mean—"

"Good job, Whitby. I'll be sure to write a letter to management, telling them how helpful you've been. The key, if you please."

The clerk hesitated. "Perhaps I should explain, Mr. Mc-Kenna. This suite is unique. Quite costly."

"It's kind of you to show concern, Whitby, but we'll take it."

"Yes, sir. But the reason it's unique is because—"

"Don't tell me." Griffin grinned and leaned closer. "What is it? The Presidential Suite?"

The clerk looked from Griffin to Dana. She could almost feel his distress, especially when their eyes met. Was that a bell ringing in the distance, or was the warning sound tolling only in her ears?

"Not exactly, sir," Mr. Whitby said, and cleared his throat. "It's—it's the Bridal Suite."

"It's only a name," Griffin said as he marched Dana across the lobby toward the elevator. "It's meaningless."

"It is not meaningless," she insisted. "If it were, they'd call it Room 2010 or Suite 2010. Something. Anything. But they wouldn't call it the Bridal Suite."

"It's a hotel, Anderson. They call suites all kinds of things. If George Washington slept in every place named for him, the guy wouldn't have had time to be President."

"I don't care what you say, McKenna. I'm not going to stay in a bridal suite with you."

They stopped before a bank of mirrored elevators. Griffin pushed the call button.

"Who's going to know it's the bridal suite, unless we tell them? Look, we've been all through this. You heard what the man said. They have no other rooms."

"There are other hotels."

"Yes. Yes, there are. But the conference is being held at this hotel. The meetings will be here. The presentations. The people we've come fifteen hundred miles to see." He shot her a cold smile. "Startling as this may sound, this is the hotel we need to stay at."

"Not in the Bridal Suite, we don't."

"Will you forget that stupid name? You were there. You heard me ask Whitby what, exactly, that name meant. And he said it didn't mean a thing"

"He did not say that," Dana said coldly.

"He didn't have to. I mean, he spelled it out, didn't he? He told us there's a bedroom—"

"One bedroom," she said, glaring at him.

"One bedroom, and a big living room with a sofa." Griffin's smile glittered as the elevator doors slid open. "You won't mind sleeping on a sofa, will you?"

There wasn't a way in hell she was going to give him the benefit of a response. "And there's only one bathroom," she said as they stepped inside the car. "One bathroom, McKenna, do you understand?"

"One bathroom's all we need," Griffin said. An elderly

couple tottered into the elevator. The doors whisked closed. "Not that I like the thought of sharing it. Having to shove aside a curtain of unmentionables so I can take my morning shower isn't my idea of a good time."

Dana shot a quick look at the elevator's two other occupants. They were facing straight ahead, but she could almost see their ears rotating in her direction.

"For your information," she said in a low voice, "I do not hang a curtain of unmentionables in the bathroom."

"No?"

"No."

"What do you do with them, then? Wash them and take them to bed with you?"

"I hang my things neatly on the towel rod—not that it's any of your business."

"It's going to be my business, now that we're going to be sharing the bridal suite." His smile glittered. "Amazing, isn't it? Here we are, about to spend the night together and until yesterday, I hardly knew you."

The old couple turned and stared at Dana, who felt her cheeks begin to burn. "It's not what you think," she stammered. "We aren't—we haven't—"

"For shame," the woman said.

Her husband put his hand on her arm. "Now, Maude, times have changed."

"Some things *never* change, Harold. Young lady, you give that young man what he wants before he puts a wedding ring on your finger and you might as well forget about him marrying you."

"But I don't want him to marry me!" Dana bit her lip. "You don't understand. He and I—"

By some merciful twist of fate, the elevator arrived at their floor. The doors slid open. Dana rushed out of the car and spun toward Griffin as he followed after her.

"That was not funny! If you think I'm going to spend the weekend letting you make crude jokes..." Dana frowned. Griffin was looking over her shoulder, and the expression on his face made the hair rise on the back of her neck. "What's the matter?"

"Look," he muttered.

Dana turned around. A low moan rose in her throat.

There was a door at the end of the hallway. It was set in splendid isolation and flanked by a pair of tables that bore gilded vases overflowing with white and pink roses. Dana's eyes widened. Surely this was a joke. Nobody would really make tables that used chubby, rosy-bottomed cherubs for supports.

But somebody had, just as somebody had seen to it that the door bore a gleaming brass plaque. Even at this distance, the engraved words stood out.

"No," Dana whispered.

Griffin gave a choked laugh. He held up the key to their suite, looked at the room number, then looked at the plaque.

"I'm afraid so," he said. "Welcome to the Bridal Suite."

CHAPTER SEVEN

DANA stood ankle-deep in the white carpet that flowed from one end of the bridal suite to the other and told herself to try and stay calm.

Inhale, she told herself. Exhale. Harmonize the body, mind and spirit. Just the way *Sensei* O'Malley had taught her to do. The idea of Tai Chi Chuan, he'd told his students, was to find your center. Your inner core. Your source of strength and serenity.

She shut her eyes and put her hands on her diaphragm.

"Breathe in," she whispered. "Breathe out. In. Out. In..."

"What in hell are you doing?"

Dana blinked her eyes open. Griffin was staring at her as if she'd lost her mind.

"I'm—I'm centering," she said.

"Centering." His mouth twitched. "It looks more like you're hyperventilating."

"Don't be silly. I never..." The room began to spin and turn gray.

"Hey!" He reached out and encircled her waist with his arm. "That's all I need right now, Anderson, is you passing out on me."

"I am not passing out," she said weakly. "I, ah, I just felt—"

"Like passing out. It's what comes of puffing in and out like a locomotive. Here, sit down."

Dana looked at the sofa he was leading her toward. It was shaped like a crescent, covered with a silky-white fabric and strewn with red, heart-shaped pillows. It looked deep enough to consume anybody who was foolish enough to dent one of its overstuffed cushions.

She shuddered and freed herself of McKenna's arm. "I'm fine, thank you."

"Yeah, well, see that you stay that way. The last thing I've got time for is a swooning female."

"I am not a swooning female, McKenna. I'll have you know, I have never fainted in my life."

"Good. Because—" Griffin's mouth snapped shut as he looked past her. "Wow. Just look at this place! Did you ever see anything like it?"

"No," Dana said. "That was why I was, uh, centering."

Griffin cackled. There was no other word to describe it. Not that she could blame him. She felt as if they'd followed Dorothy straight into the land of Oz.

"The guy who did the decorating must have been whacked out," he said. "It's incredible."

Incredible was an understatement. Dana frowned. Maybe she was dreaming. Or hallucinating. She'd done that once, when she was a little girl. Her mother had taken her to a free dental clinic and the dentist—dental student, she'd realized, years after—had given her what he'd said would be a whiff of gas. But he must have given her too much because the next thing she'd known, blue monkeys had been hanging from the ceiling.

A simple hallucinatory episode, they'd told her, after they'd brought her around. Not so simple, Dana had thought, and not only because the fear in the student's eyes had contradicted his words but because she'd been terrified, seeing things she knew weren't really there.

Not this time. This—all of it—was real.

"Heart-shaped pillows," Griffin said. "Do you believe it?"

He was holding out one of the red pillows, grinning at her as if he expected her to share in the joke.

"Tacky," she said with a little smile.

"Tacky's a start." He tossed the pillow on the sofa and strolled through the room, pausing every now and then to take a closer look at one thing or another. "Look at this, Anderson.

Champagne flutes and a little card saying there's a bottle of bubbly in the bar refrigerator.''

"How nice," she said politely. "We can offer it to our first guests."

"Yeah. And get this. A stereo, complete with CDs." He chuckled. "Mood music."

"Mood music," she echoed. "How...lovely."

"And a VCR," Griffin bent down and peered at the video-tapes lined up neatly on a shelf. "*Casablanca. An Affair to Remember.* And something called *The Way We Were.*" He frowned. "Must be an old one."

Dana nodded. "Oh, it is. It..."

She swallowed hard. What was the matter with her? A suite, Whitby had said. A bridal suite. She'd known what to expect, something schmaltzy and saccharine. Well, the furnishings were all that, and more. The decor was overblown, and a little embarrassing, and she wanted to laugh it off, the way Griffin was doing—except she couldn't. If these were all just silly fripperies, why was her throat constricting as she listened to Griffin read the names of those romantic old movies?

"Oh, hell."

She looked up. Griffin had made his way further into the living room. He'd opened a door, to what she supposed was a closet or maybe the bedroom, and stepped inside. Now, he looked over his shoulder at her.

"Wait until you see this."

"What?" she said with false gaiety.

"Come look. Trust me, Anderson, there's no way I can do this justice."

Dana pasted a smile to her lips. "What is it? The bedroo... Ohmygod," she said as she looked past his shoulder.

"My sentiments, to the letter. Can you believe it?"

She couldn't, no. She had never even imagined a bathroom could look like this. And to think she'd been concerned about the intimacy of sharing. Oh, it boggled the mind.

"Pink marble," Griffin said. He whistled in admiration. "A shower stall that could host a party of six."

"Eight," Dana said gaily, though her eyes were riveted not on the shower but on the tub—if you wanted to call the heart-shaped thing a tub.

Nobody would ever just take a bath in it, that was certain.

It was pink marble, too, sunk into a small jungle of flowers and ferns, and bathed in the soft glow of recessed spotlights. A second pair of champagne flutes was within easy reach of the rim, standing alongside an assortment of bath oils with names like—like—

"Passion Flower," Griffin said. He bent closer to the bottles. *"Jungle Nights."* He uncorked a bottle, took a sniff of the contents. "Holy hell, Anderson. Get a whiff of this stuff."

"No." Dana jumped back, then gave a quick smile. "I, ah, I'm allergic to things like that. You know, stuff with heavy perfumes."

"Well, this is heavy, all right." He closed the bottle and set it back down on the edge of the tub. "Some layout."

"Yes, isn't it? Well, we'll work it out. The times we get to use the shower, I mean."

Griffin turned and smiled at her. It was a teasing smile, but her heart took a tumble.

"It might be more efficient to skip the shower and use the tub," he said. "There's plenty of room for two."

She knew she was blushing and she hated herself for it almost as much as she hated him for making it happen, but she stood her ground and looked him in the eye.

"I'll draw up the schedule," she said coolly, "and post it on the door. Any objections?"

"Ah, Anderson, where's your sense of adventure?"

"I prefer to shower in the morning. You can shower at night."

His smile tilted. "When does the Bow Tie take his shower?"

Dammit, he was making her blush again!

"My fiancé's bathing habits are none of your business, Mr. McKenna."

"You're engaged?"

"We're as good as engaged, and that's not any of your business, either."

Griffin's eyes darkened. "If you were my fiancée," he said softly, "I'd be damned if I'd let you go away with another man for a weekend."

"I am not away with another man, I am away with you. This is strictly business. Arthur knows that. Well, he will, just as soon as I call him."

"Yeah," Griffin folded his arms and leaned back against the wall. "I noticed."

"Noticed what? Really, Mr. McKenna, I'd like to see my bedroom, and unpack." She caught her breath as Griffin reached out his hand and lazily stroked a finger across her cheekbone.

"You never phoned ol' Arthur."

"I just said—"

"I offered you a job, and all you could think of was upping the ante." His smile was as lazy as the whisper of his hand against her throat. "Now, if you were my fiancée, I'd expect you to think of me before you thought of hopping on a plane and heading out of state for a long weekend with another guy."

"Will you stop that?" Dana said irritably as she brushed his hand aside. "You were the one who kept saying there was no time to waste, McKenna. And, I repeat, I have not gone off for a long weekend with another man. You are not—"

"Careful, Anderson." Griffin chuckled softly. "If you're going to impugn my manhood, you'd better be prepared for me to prove you wrong."

Their eyes met, their gazes locked.

"You enjoy this," Dana said in a low, angry voice. "You get a kick out of embarrassing me."

"Is that what I'm doing? Embarrassing you?"

"You know you are!"

Griffin frowned. She had him there. That was exactly what he was doing. And she had every right to be ticked off. There was no reason to be teasing her. Teasing a woman, especially this kind of double entendre stuff, was just another way of flirting, and he didn't flirt with the women he worked with; he never had. It was a bad business practice. It was just that it was so damned easy to get a rise out of her.

Maybe it was because she was so serious, or because she had a kind of naïveté he hardly ever saw in a career-minded woman. In any kind of woman, in today's insane world.

"If this place makes you feel uncomfortable, McKenna, don't take it out on me!"

"Don't be ridiculous," he said coldly, although he knew, instantly, that she was right. The suite *did* make him uncomfortable, which was silly, but he'd be damned if he'd let her know that. He was in charge. He was in complete control.

"It's time to get the show on the road." He shouldered past her, collected their luggage from near the door, and strode the length of the living room. "We'll unpack, hang our stuff away—"

"Forget the use of the plural," Dana said as she hurried after him. "*We* are not unpacking. We are not hanging anything away. I get the bedroom, you get the living room."

"Bedrooms have closets, Anderson." Griffin paused outside the door of what had to be the bedroom. "And," he said, shouldering it open, "the closet is where I intend to park my stuff. If you think..."

His voice died away.

"McKenna? What's wrong now?"

He gave a strangled laugh. "Prepare yourself," he said, and held out his hand.

Dana looked at the hand, ignored it, took a deep, centering breath and stepped inside the bedroom.

"Nothing could surprise me," she said, "after that bathroom..." Her breath caught. "Oh, my," she whispered.

"Uh-huh. That just about sums it up."

He was wrong, Dana thought. Nothing could sum it up. If the living room was straight out of the land of Oz, the bedroom was—it was—

"The Arabian nights," Griffin said softly.

Dana looked at him. "Yes. You're right. It's—it's—"

Tacky, she'd almost said, but not even she could pull off such a lie. The simple truth was that this was the stuff of middle-of-the-night dreams. Two walls were draped in pale pink silk; one was all glass and overlooked the ocean. The fourth wall was mirrored and faced the bed—a bed covered in pale pink silk and shielded in yards of frothy white lace.

"Damn," Griffin said very softly.

He turned to her. She could see him reflected in the mirrored panels, a dozen Griffin McKennas, each of them looking at her in a way that made her heart stand still. Their eyes met, and the room filled with silence. No, not silence. Dana could hear a roaring in her ears. It was like an ocean. Yes. Yes, it had to be the sound of the ocean, hurling itself against the beach down below...

"Dana."

Griffin whispered her name. She felt it brush like a feather down her spine, and she knew that the roaring she heard was the sound of her blood racing through her veins.

"No," she said...but as she said it, she was moving toward him, or he was moving toward her, she didn't know which, she only knew that suddenly they were in each other's arms.

"No, Griffin."

The words were a lie. Even as he bent to her, she was lifting herself to him, slipping her arms around his neck, tunneling her hands into his hair, offering him her mouth.

Offering him everything.

He groaned, cupped his hand behind her head, and took her mouth. His kiss was hungry, hot and urgent. There was no tenderness to it, but tenderness wasn't what she wanted. She wanted him, had wanted him for days. For all the years of her life, and when he caught her up in his arms and took her to the bed, she sighed and sank down with him into the softness of the silk, her hands already under his shirt, her fingers hot against his hard, muscled flesh, her mouth open to his.

"Dana," he whispered, as if her name were all he could manage. He tried to pull back, so he could undress her, but she clung to him, whispering his name, kissing him with a hunger she'd never known before. His hand closed on her blouse, tore it, ripped it from her, exposing her flesh to his mouth, his hungry, eager mouth...

Somewhere in the distance, bells began to ring, chiming out the opening notes of *Here Comes the Bride*.

It was the doorbell.

They went rigid in each other's arms. The bells rang again. Griffin cursed, rolled off the bed, and headed for the front door.

Dana sat up. She was trembling. What had she done? What had she *almost* done? She got to her feet, dragged the ragged edges of her blouse together and tried to think. She could hear voices in the living room. Griffin's, rough and angry. Another man's—Mr. Whitby's?—apologetic and unctuous.

A sob burst from her throat. Frantic, she spun in a tight circle. There had to be a closet. A hall. Someplace where she could hide, where she could fix her hair, her blouse...

"It was the manager."

Dana swung toward the doorway. Griffin looked at her, his expression cool. She pulled her jacket over her gaping blouse, but his eyes were fixed to her face.

"He wanted to know..." He gave a harsh laugh. "He wanted to know if we were satisfied."

She felt color race up under her skin. "Satisfied?" she said dumbly.

"Yes. You know, were the accommodations okay, did we have enough towels..." A muscle tightened in his cheek. "I told him we couldn't stay here."

Dana nodded jerkily. "Good."

"I told him that there was no way we could entertain clients in this setting."

She nodded again. It was all she seemed capable of doing. Her brain felt numb; she stared at Griffin, wondering how he could manage to look so unruffled, sound so calm, as if they were having a meeting in the office, as if they hadn't—as if they hadn't just been—

"I said that I wasn't born yesterday, that I knew damned well that hotels always had a couple of rooms stashed away to take care of the overflow, or of some VIP who might come through the door at the last minute."

"And?" Dana cleared her throat. "And, what did he say?"

Just for an instant, something seemed to flicker under that calm facade.

"He was one step ahead of me. He said that these *were* the overflow rooms, and that if any VIP came along, they'd just have to put him in the broom closet." He paused. "So, I said that we'd do the best we could, under the circumstances."

"No!" Dana almost shouted the word. "Forget it, Mc-Kenna. I will not stay in this—"

"Listen to me, Dana."

"There's nothing you can say that will change my mind. What just happened—what damn near happened..."

"Nothing happened."

She stared at him. He looked as if he'd been hewn from stone, his face set, his eyes icy-blue. The man who stood before her was Griffin McKenna, the corporate raider, and for the first time, she understood why he was respected—and feared.

"Nothing happened," he repeated.

It was silly, but the dismissive words stung her.

"You can't just pretend—"

"I'm not pretending." He walked toward her and she told herself not to shrink back against the wall. "I'm simply stating facts. We're both tired, and this damned pleasure palace isn't exactly conducive to sainthood." His mouth hardened. "In other words, you're a woman and I'm a man. And, despite what our politically correct pundits say, there are differences between the sexes."

Dana drew herself up. "Now just a minute, McKenna—"

"Spare me the dialectic, Anderson. I'm not about to debate the issue. The bottom line is that things got out of hand a minute ago, but it won't happen again."

"You're damned right it won't."

"Sexual attraction can be controlled, the same as any other emotion."

"I agree, McKenna."

Griffin smiled thinly. "Do you suppose we might move on to addressing each other by our first names? Considering our relationship, I mean. Our business relationship," he said when he saw her eyes flash a warning. "I'll call you Dana, you'll call me Griffin. It's the practice I follow with the people who work with me. As for the rest..." He waved a hand toward the bed in a clear gesture of dismissal. "Just put it out of your mind."

"Just put it..."

"You can do that, can't you?"

His voice was hard, and dangerous. What was he worried about? Did he think he was so irresistible that he'd have to spend the weekend fending her off? Well, he could relax. What had happened a little while ago had been the price she'd paid for the highs and lows of the past couple of days. It wasn't all that different from looking up and seeing blue monkeys.

"Yes."

"Good. I'm glad we have that out of the way."

"Yes. So am I. And now, if you don't mind—Griffin—I'd like to unpack."

"Certainly."

"I'm sure you'll understand, though, if I suggest you unpack in the living room."

"No problem."

Dana smiled politely, and waited for Griffin to step aside. He didn't.

"Ah, if you wouldn't mind? You're standing in my way."

"Oh."

He didn't move. She cleared her throat. "Griffin. Step aside, please."

"You're sure you followed what I said? About there being nothing to be concerned about?"

"Of course," she said quickly, looking up at him. Had he

moved closer? His eyes were dark. So dark. Her heart gave a crazy thump.

"Sexual appetite," he muttered. His gaze fell to her mouth. "Easily controlled, especially since you're not my type of woman anyway, Anderson."

"Well, you're not my type of man, McKenna." Her heart thumped again. His hand was slipping up her throat, his fingers threading deep into her hair. What had happened to the clips that kept it off her face? What was happening to her knees? "Not my type at—"

His mouth closed on hers, very gently. She made a soft little sound; she lifted her hand, almost touched his chest, then drew it back down to her side.

Griffin lifted his head.

"It was just an aberration," he whispered. "Understood?"

Dana nodded. "Understood." Her hand rose again and this time she touched him, lay her palm flat against his chest and felt the gallop of his heart. He hissed, caught her hand in his, and brought it to his lips. "An aberration." Her voice shook.

"Of course," he said. He tilted her face up to his and kissed her again, slowly, passionately, his mouth open, the tip of his tongue playing against the tip of hers.

She shuddered. "Of course," she sighed, and sucked his tongue into her mouth.

He groaned. His hands slid down and down, cupped her bottom and lifted her into him. He was fully, excitingly aroused; she felt the thrust of him against her belly and she rose up on her toes and curled her fingers into his lapels.

They drew back at the same moment, the flush on her face mirroring on his. The seconds slipped by while they stared into each other's eyes, and then Griffin took a shuddering breath.

"I'm going to go down to the lobby. You know, look around, see who else has checked in." He touched the back of his hand to the hollow of her throat. "All right?"

"Yes."

He nodded. "Good. Good." He spoke quietly, as if nothing

had happened. But his hand was still at her throat, as if measuring the flutter of her pulse. "Meet me in the bar at six. Can you manage that?"

"Seven," she said. She could feel her heartbeat slowing as he took his hand away. "That'll give me time to follow through on some of the code work I did on the plane."

"Seven. Fine." He stepped back. "Anderson?"

Dana cleared her throat. "Yes?"

For a long, long moment, he didn't speak. Then he cupped her face in one hand and kissed her again, with a sweet, yearning tenderness that made her dizzy.

"If that door has a lock," he said gruffly, "use it when you go to bed tonight."

He walked from the room. She waited until she was sure her knees wouldn't buckle. Then, carefully, she shut the door. There was a lock. She looked at it, considered, and turned it, although she was no longer sure whether it was to keep Griffin out or to keep her in. Then she crossed the room, sat down gingerly on the edge of the bed and took a deep breath.

Finally, she reached for the phone and dialed.

"Mr. Coakley, please," she said, and when she heard Arthur's familiar voice, she almost sobbed with relief.

"Arthur," she began cheerfully, "I'm afraid I won't be able to keep our dinner appointment this evening. You'll never guess where I am..."

CHAPTER EIGHT

GRIFFIN sat in the Coconut Lounge of the Hotel de las Palmas and wondered if he'd gone crazy.

How else to explain what he'd just done?

He was an adult male. Sophisticated. Intelligent. In full and complete control of his emotions, manners, and hormones.

That's what he'd been, anyway, until he'd come on to Dana with all the subtlety of a stallion in heat.

Griffin reached for his bourbon and water, lifted it halfway to his lips, then set it down. Booze was the last thing he needed. A bucket of ice water, was more like it. Or maybe a quick trip to a psychiatrist's couch.

Tell me, Doctor, why would a man who has his pick of women—hey, this was not a time for false modesty—why would such a man try and bed the one woman in the entire world who least appeals to him?

It was an excellent question. Griffin looked at his drink, frowned, picked it up and then put it down again.

Why, indeed?

He had no idea. And, he suspected, neither would the eminent shrink.

"Hell," he muttered.

"Sir?"

Griffin looked up. The bartender smiled politely.

"Did you want something?"

"No. Yes." Griffin frowned. "I suppose people sit here day after day, telling you the damnedest stories."

"Oh, they do, sir. They do, indeed."

"Men probably talk about women, women about men...?"

"It's the men who do most of the talking, sir."

Griffin nodded. "Women are almost a different species, aren't they?"

The bartender chuckled. "You can say that again."

Griffin sighed. He pushed his drink aside. "Ditch the bourbon," he said. "Bring me a club soda, with a twist of lemon."

"Very good, sir. Anything else?"

A functional brain, Griffin thought. "No, just the club soda."

He nodded his thanks when the soda was set before him, lifted the glass and took a long swallow.

What had happened, up there in the bridal suite? Why had he kissed Dana Anderson?

Kissed her? Griffin almost laughed. He hadn't kissed her, he'd damn near ravaged her, or he would have, given another thirty seconds.

No. Ravaged wasn't the right word, not unless Dana wanted to admit that she'd done her share of ravaging, too. Touching her had been like touching a ribbon of flame. He'd never experienced anything like it. The way her mouth had clung to his. The way she'd melted into him, uttered those soft little cries that had almost driven him past the point of no return.

The glass shook in Griffin's hand. He put it down, carefully, and took a deep breath.

Back to square one. Maybe he *was* crazy. Or maybe she was. For all he knew, they were a scientific phenomenon, two seemingly rational human beings who'd suddenly gone over the edge together.

The only certainty was that he'd never done anything like that in his life. He was a man who liked women; he took great pleasure in uninhibited, passionate sex—but he was always in control. Always.

Until the Anderson woman came into his life.

Bringing her here had been dumb. He should have remembered how things had gone in his office yesterday. He hadn't been any more in control then than he had in that ridiculous bedroom just now. If he had any brains at all, he'd have...

Hell.

If, if, if. Should have. Would have. Could have.

Griffin picked up the glass and drank some of the club soda. What was it Dana had said? Something about everybody making it to heaven if "if" ruled the world?

She was right. What was done, was done. The thing to do now was put the foolishness behind him and get on with business.

So she was attractive, once you got past the funny hair and the shapeless outfits. Big deal. He had the numbers of most of New York's most beautiful women in his address book. What was attractive, compared to that?

"Nothing," he muttered. "Nothing at all."

Was she sexy? Was she flirty? Did she look at him with stars in her eyes?

"No," Griffin muttered.

No, she sure as hell didn't. Wasn't. Whatever. She'd said he wasn't her type, and she certainly wasn't his. Okay, maybe she had possibilities, but so what? Basically, she had about as much femininity to her as an audit report.

"Hi."

Griffin looked around. A woman was sliding onto the stool beside his. Nice, he thought. Very nice. Long, straight red hair. An oval face. Big, dark eyes and a pouting mouth that made his imagination sit up and take notice.

She smiled. "Are you here for the conference?"

Her voice was low and sultry. She was wearing a black dress, some sort of backless, sleeveless thing. Her breasts oozed from the bodice like ripe fruit. She smiled, leaned back a little and crossed her legs.

A little obvious, not as subtly sexy as Anderson, but...

Griffin frowned, emptied his head of such nonsense and told himself that he was about to be a very lucky man.

"Yes," he said, smiling back at her. "And you?"

She nodded. "I'm with Omniplex Computers." She held out her hand. "Julie Everett."

He took her hand, held it a second longer than manners

required. A weight seemed to lift from his shoulders. It was going to be a pleasant weekend, after all.

"Hello, Julie Everett. I'm—"

"Sir?"

Griffin looked up. The bartender held out a telephone. "Sorry to interrupt, Mr. McKenna."

Griffin sighed. "A call?"

"Yes, sir."

"Yeah, okay." He took the phone and shot the redhead a quick smile. "You just hold that thought, Julie Everett."

Her brows lifted. "What thought?"

"The one I hope we're sharing, about the rest of the evening."

She laughed. It was a nice laugh, soft and musical, and pleasant to hear. Griffin felt his spirits lift. This was the way women were supposed to be. Sweet. Compliant. Eager to please...

"McKenna?"

Dana's angry bark sounded in his ear. He winked at the redhead, turned away, and spoke into the phone.

"Anderson. What's the problem?"

"I'll tell you the problem. You are the problem."

Griffin scowled at the phone. "Listen, Anderson, is this really important? Because if it can wait—"

"You had to have things your own way, didn't you?"

"I already apologized for that," he said, lowering his voice. "There's no need to—"

"I'll put my carry-on under my seat, I said. 'Oh, no,' you said. 'Give it to me,' you said. 'I'll put it into the overhead compartment.'"

"What the hell are you talking about?"

"My luggage. What does it sound like I'm talking about?"

"What about your luggage? Dammit, Anderson—"

"It isn't."

"Isn't what?"

"Isn't my carry-on," Dana said impatiently. "It looks like

mine. It's the same size and color, but when I opened it up, it was full of some guy's dirty laundry.''

Griffin sighed. Just what he needed. A luggage screwup.

"Okay," he said, "okay, I'll report it to the airline."

"I'm not helpless, McKenna. I already did that."

"And? I assume they've already heard from the guy who took your carry-on by mistake. Let them send somebody over to make the switch."

"Assuming anything is a mistake, McKenna. Didn't the screwups with the code and the hotel reservations teach you that?"

Griffin felt a faint hammering begin in his temples. "You're right. Forget what I said. Just get to the bottom line."

"The bottom line is that I don't have my luggage, and neither does the airline. The flight continued on to Bogota. My clothes are probably sitting inside a hut beside the Amazon River by now."

He shut his eyes, blinked them open, and looked toward the ceiling. "The Amazon doesn't come anywhere near Bogota."

"Dammit, I don't care! I want my luggage!"

"All right, calm down. These things happen. Look, I saw a shop in the lobby where I'm sure you can pick up whatever you need. Come down, buy what you want, and bill it to me."

"I can't do that."

"Don't be an idiot. It's not as if I'm offering to set you up in an apartment."

The redhead chose that instant to move into his line of vision. One glance, and he knew she'd heard the last sentence.

Griffin slapped his hand over the telephone.

"It's not what you think," he said quickly.

"You just hold that thought," she said with a little smile.

Dana's voice buzzed from the handset. Griffin ignored it. He watched the redhead's slow exit and the collapse of his plans for the evening. Jaw set, he turned his back to the door and jammed the phone against his ear.

"You have five minutes to get your tail down to that shop,

Anderson. Five minutes. If not, your job is history. Do I make myself clear?''

"Whatever you say, McKenna." Her voice trembled with anger. "I just hope you're ready to explain to anybody who asks why I'm down there, walking around in clothes that look like they've been ripped off."

"All right. Okay, you've made your point. Stay where you are. I'll take care of everything."

"I don't want you to take care of everything. I just want you to get me something to wear."

"I'll do that, and I'll have it sent up."

"Thank you."

Griffin almost laughed. Anne Boleyn must have said the same kind of "thank you" to the executioner who'd assured her that the blade of his ax was razor-sharp.

"Tell me what you need," he said.

"I need everything. Toothbrush. Toothpaste. Comb."

"Try that stage set of a bathroom. There's bound to be an assortment of toiletries in there."

"You're right. I'm using the portable phone. Let me just walk down and check... Okay, scratch the toothbrush and stuff. Just get me something to wear for this evening. I'll stay here and work on the code until it's time to meet you, and I'll do the rest of my shopping tomorrow."

"Sounds good," Griffin signaled to the bartender for a pencil and paper. "Size?"

Dana hesitated. He could almost see her trying to find a way not to give him such personal information.

"Come on, Anderson. What's the matter? Are you afraid I'll make a wax doll in a size twelve and stick pins in it?"

"Eight," she said coldly. "I'm size eight."

He grinned. "Eight. Fine. I'll pick out a feed sack and have it sent up."

"Very amusing. Just get me something simple, please."

"I'll do my best."

"A man-tailored blouse. White, with long sleeves."

"I just said, I'll do my best."

"And a suit. Or a skirt and a blazer, if they don't have a suit. Something conservative."

"Anderson, I am not the Saks Personal Shopper."

"Tell the salesclerk I want a skirt that falls below the knee. Either that, or trousers. Tweed is good, if they have it, or a lightweight wool. Oh, and I prefer a dark color—"

Griffin hung up.

The Shoppe de Mer was just off the lobby. The display window held an assortment of gold and silver balloons, a stuffed flamingo and a couple of bathing suits that gave him pause. He'd seen stuff like that on the Cote d'Azur, but could a woman really wear two circles of silk and a thong in the good old U.S. of A. and get away with it?

Regretfully, he thought about how terrific Julie Whatever-Her-Name-Was would look in something like that...

Dana would look even better.

Griffin frowned and stepped inside.

The salesclerk, ageless and elegant, went with the territory. He doubted if the word "tweed" would be either in her vocabulary or in the shop's back room, but he gave it his best shot.

"Tweed?" she said as if she'd just gotten a mouthful of lemon juice.

"Tweed," he said pleasantly. "You know—scratchy wool, the kind favored by spinster great-aunts. In a size eight."

Her smile assured him that she was willing to share in the joke.

"I know the fabric, sir, but I'm afraid there's little call for something so—traditional, in South Beach."

Griffin nodded as he strolled around the little shop. Surprisingly enough, he'd never been in a place like this before. He never bought his women gifts of clothing. Flowers, yes, and perfume, and jewelry sometimes, but never clothing.

Clothing was far too personal...but it surely was interesting.

"What's this?" he said, nodding at a bit of pale blue silk.

"That's a camisole, sir. Does the lady in question prefer camisoles to bras?"

Did she? Griffin thought back to the morning. He was pretty certain Dana hadn't been wearing anything under that Lois Lane sweatshirt. She wouldn't need to—he'd felt the round fullness of her breasts against his chest, felt their lush firmness...

"Sir?"

Griffin blinked. "I'll take it," he said gruffly.

"We have matching panties, too," She held up two snippets of silk. "Which would madam prefer, do you think? The tap pants? Or the thong?"

Madam would prefer to club me over the head, Griffin thought, especially if I buy her undies.

"Oh, the thong," he said. "Definitely."

"There's a matching garter belt, of course."

"Of course," he said calmly.

"And hose. Would madam wish a pale shade? Nude, perhaps?"

Damn, what had he gotten himself into? Nude was not a concept he wanted to consider right now. He could almost see Dana wearing nothing but the camisole, the thong panties, the garter belt and the sheer-as-a-cobweb stockings...

"Nude." His voice cracked, and he cleared his throat. "Nude, would be fine."

The clerk nodded. "You did say madam prefers suits?"

"Suits," Griffin said, forcing his attention back to the business at hand. "Uh, yes. She likes suits, but I believe we've already established that you have nothing in tweed."

"I have a silk suit that might be just right."

"In a size eight?"

"Indeed. Let me show it to you."

The clerk drew something from a rack. The sexy underwear, the bathing suits in the window, the clingy, soft garments hanging all around the shop had put Griffin's brain into overdrive. The thing on the hanger brought him quickly back to reality. It was a suit, made of silk but in a flat white that reminded him of the underbelly of a dead fish. The skirt was long enough to please a nun, and the jacket was big enough to shelter at least two people.

He hated it on sight. Dana would love it.

"Would you call this suit conservative?" he asked.

The clerk gave him a strange look, but he figured she had the right, considering that a man with his taste in underwear would ask such a thing.

"I suppose so," she said slowly.

He nodded. What was the sense in fantasizing? Dana would sooner wear a blanket than anything he might buy in this shop. She wanted conservative? She could have conservative.

"Great. Send it to—" To the Bridal Suite, he'd almost said, but his lips wouldn't form the words. "To Suite 2010. And put it on my account."

"What about shoes, sir?"

"Shoes?" He looked blank. "She—the lady has shoes. Black ones, if I remember right. Conservative, like the suit. You know, those things with chunky, low heels... What?"

The clerk cleared her throat. "If I may suggest, sir..." She held up two scraps of leather, the same shade as the suit. "These would be preferable."

"Yeah, sure." Griffin was starting to feel uncomfortable. Maybe he should have told the clerk what he needed, let her pick out everything instead of doing it himself. "If you think she needs shoes, toss 'em in."

"Size?"

He ran his hand through his hair. "I don't know. She's tall. Well, not too tall. She's..."

"About my size, perhaps?"

"Yes. A couple of inches taller. And a little, ah, curvier..."

Dammit all, the clerk was trying not to smile. And he—he was blushing! Blushing, and all because a woman who didn't like being a woman had sent him to do a chore no man should ever have to do.

A scowl spread over his face.

"Send up an assortment of sizes," he said in the same tone

he used when he ordered his broker to buy ten thousand shares of stock. "One is sure to be right." He glanced at the little pile of silk wisps that Dana would never call underwear. "As for that stuff..."

"Sir?"

Forget about it, he'd been going to say, but hell, a man could dream, couldn't he?

"Send it up, too," he said, and then he scribbled his name on the bill and beat a quick retreat.

He called Dana on a house phone, told her the shop would be delivering the things she needed, and that he'd drift around the conference floor for the rest of the afternoon and meet her in the lobby at seven, as they'd planned.

At six forty-five, he settled in to wait. She'd been fast as lightning this morning, and he had no reason to expect otherwise now. Women didn't tell time the same way men did, that was a fact of life, but Dana didn't live by female rules.

The minutes slipped by. Griffin glanced at the big wall clock over the elevators and frowned. Twenty after seven. Where was she? There was a cocktail party this evening, for the conference attendees, followed by a rubber-chicken dinner. It was the kind of thing he hated but he knew it had to be endured. He'd do some networking and leave the computer talk to Dana. He wondered if she'd made any headway with the code. She'd only been at it a couple of hours, but still...

Griffin felt his heart stop. A woman stepped hesitantly from the elevator, one he'd never seen before—one he knew he had wanted, all his life.

Dana.

No wonder the salesclerk had looked at him as if he were crazy when he'd asked her if the silk suit was conservative. Conservative? He'd have laughed at his own stupidity, if he could have trusted himself to do anything more complicated than to get to his feet and stare.

Everything he'd thought about the suit had been wrong. It was ivory, not white, a shade that brought out the rosy blush in Dana's skin and made her tumble of loose curls gleam like gold. The jacket he'd thought was big was, instead, clingy and sexy. It tied at the waist—such a sweet, slender waist—and the single tie was all that held the jacket together. Beneath, he could see the creamy length of Dana's throat, and the gentle rise of her breasts.

And the skirt. Griffin's throat tightened. What an idiot he was to have thought it concealing. The skirt was long, yes...long and clinging. It was slit all the way from the narrow hem to her thigh.

A hush fell over the lobby. People were looking. Griffin felt his heart swell with anticipation as he started toward Dana. He wanted to sweep her into his arms and tell every man whose eyes were popping that this beautiful woman was his.

His? But she wasn't his. He didn't want her to be his.

Did he?

"Griffin?"

Her voice, soft and wonderfully sweet, made his pulse quicken. They were standing only inches apart. Dana's head was tilted back. Her eyes were glittering, her lips were parted. Griffin gave up the fight. Of course, he wanted her. And she wanted him. He could see it in the way she was staring at him, with an intensity that sent a tingle right down to his toes.

"Yes," he said softly, and flashed a killer smile.

It could work. First this long weekend, then a lazy affair back in the city. A month, maybe even two...

"Griffin," she said, "if we were alone—"

Every muscle in his body tightened. He could feel the eroticism of the moment, sense the words of need and desire she was going to whisper right here in this crowded, public place.

"If we were alone, Griffin, I'd smile while I killed you."

He blinked.

"I asked for tweed."

"They didn't have tweed."

"I asked for conservative."

"They told me this was conservative."

"I've never worn anything so—so—"

"Feminine?"

"Revealing. I'm positive everyone is staring."

"They are." Amazing, he thought, that he could carry on such a rational conversation when what he wanted was to sling this gorgeous creature over his shoulder and carry her off. "You look—you look—"

Her hand snaked out between them and she jabbed him in the gut.

"And what's with the..." Her cheeks turned crimson. "The underwear?"

Griffin slid an arm around her waist. "Could we discuss this someplace else?"

"We can discuss it right here."

"Well," he said pleasantly, "in that case, you need to speak just a little bit louder. That gentleman to your right is having trouble keeping up with the conversation."

Dana looked to the side. Her cheeks turned a deep crimson, and she let Griffin lead her through the lobby to an alcove hidden behind a pair of potted palms.

"Answer the question," she snapped, twisting out of his encircling arm. "Why on earth did you buy me that underwear?"

He shrugged. "I figured you needed some."

"I didn't. I was wearing perfectly adequate..." The wash of color swept over her face again. "You know what I mean. What you selected was—outrageous."

"It was the only stuff they had." It wasn't really a lie; it was the only stuff he'd seen, but why mention that? His gaze moved over her, lingering for a heartbeat on her mouth before rising, again, so that their eyes met. "So, tell me."

"Tell you what?"

He smiled lazily. "Do you have those things on?"

"Do I have..." Dana lifted her chin. "It's none of your business."

He smiled, and her breath caught at the dangerous promise in that smile.

"Meaning, you do."

"Meaning just what I said, McKenna. It's none of your business—but if I do, it's only because I showered, and I couldn't just put on the stuff I'd worn all day."

"Showered?" He lifted a hand, touched it to her shoulder. The silk of the suit sighed under his fingertips. He could feel the heat of her skin, burning like fire through its softness. "I figured you'd use that big tub." His hand stroked across her shoulder, slid gently under her hair and around the nape of her neck.

Dana swallowed hard. "Don't change the subject! You had no right to buy me any of that stuff."

He grinned. "Wanted to murder me the second you saw it, did you?"

"It won't work, McKenna."

"What? The underwear? But you already admitted you were wearing—"

"This—this childish plan of yours." His fingers moved lightly against her skin. Oh, she thought, how good it felt, having him touch her. She wanted to shut her eyes, tilt her head into his palm, purr like a kitten...

"What childish plan?"

"I am an intelligent woman, McKenna. I know what you're doing."

"Really?" Griffin's eyes were dark, almost blurred with passion. He moved closer to her; she took a step back until her shoulders were against the wall. "That's good, Anderson. That's very good, because I sure as hell don't know what I'm doing."

"You do. You're trying to... Don't do that!"

"I'm just sniffing you, that's all." He bent his head. His nose, then his mouth, brushed the sensitive skin just behind her ear. "What's that scent?"

"It's..." God, her knees were buckling! "It's bath oil. It was in that basket in the bathroom."

"I thought you said you didn't use the tub."

"I didn't. I rubbed the oil on after I..."

"Rubbed it on?" He moved again, so that his body was

pressed lightly against hers. She could feel the heat coming off him, and the hardness of his arousal against her belly. "All over?" His voice was low, so low that it seemed to thrum through her blood. "I could have done that for you, if I'd been there."

Dana closed her eyes. "Please," she whispered, "don't."

"Don't what? I'm just trying to impress you with my usefulness."

A low moan broke from her throat. His hand was in her hair, and he was tilting her head back. Her heart was beating so quickly she was sure he could hear it pounding against her ribs.

"McKenna..."

"Griffin." He bent his head, brushed his lips over hers. "A man and a woman sharing the Bridal Suite should at least be on a first-name basis."

"Listen to me," she said desperately. "I showered because I was running late. I spent the afternoon working on the code, trying to fix it."

"Did you?"

"Yes. No. I'm not sure. I'll have to try it again, later."

"Much later."

"Dammit, Griffin! This isn't fair. I'm trying to tell you that I made progress on the code and you—you're trying to seduce me."

There was a silence, and then he drew back, just enough so he could look down into her eyes.

"You're right," he said softly. "I am."

Dana blushed. "I—I didn't expect you to—to admit it so—so—"

Griffin cupped her face in his hands. "It's too late to lie about it, Dana. We're not children. We both know what's happening."

Logic, and whatever remained of self-preservation, told her to deny the statement, but how could she, after this afternoon? How could she, when she was staring up into his eyes and trembling with longing?

"It's wrong," she said in a breathless whisper.

"Why is it wrong?"

"Because..." Why? Why was it wrong? "Because—because of that woman I saw with you in the restaurant."

"Cynthia?" He shook his head. "She's a friend, that's all,' His eyes darkened. "What about the Bow Tie? Have you really got something going with him?"

"Arthur? No. I mean, he's never said..."

Griffin drew her into his arms and kissed her. "I've never wanted a woman as I want you," he whispered. He looked into her eyes. "Be honest, Dana. You want me, just as much."

She did, he was right. And that was why it was wrong, because if she went to bed with him, she would never be able to forget him...

Griffin put his arm around her. "Come with me."

"Where?"

To bed, he wanted to say—but not yet. He wanted to draw out the pleasure, prolong the anticipation until the both of them were dizzy with hunger and wanting for each other.

"I don't know. We could take a walk, on the beach." The image blazed to life in his mind. "Maybe we could build a fire," he whispered. "And we could dance, on the sand. Do you like to dance?"

She looked up at him and smiled. "Yes. I love to—"

He bent and kissed her hungrily, and this time she rose toward him, wound her arms tightly around his neck and opened her mouth to his.

"Griffin," she whispered, and buried her hot face against his chest. "Griffin..."

She felt the swift quickening in his body. "The hell with this," he growled, and then he was turning her toward the lobby, leading her out from behind the palms. "The only place we're going is to—"

"Ohmygod!" Dana stumbled to a halt, her face suddenly as pale as her ivory suit. "Look," she whispered, and pointed a trembling finger toward the registration desk.

"What?" Griffin said irritably—and then he groaned. A

woman stood at the desk, looking flustered and lost. "Cynthia?" he muttered, his voice rising in disbelief.

Dana shoved free of his encircling arm. "Just a friend, huh?" Her voice shook. She swung toward him, eyes flashing fire. "You—you rat! What kind of man are you? Trying to seduce me when all the time, you knew that—that woman was on her way to join you for the weekend! What were you going to do? Play musical bedrooms?"

"Dana, I swear to you, I had no idea she'd be here."

"No?"

"No. Honest to—"

"So you figured you'd take a shot at me, instead?"

"She must have decided to surprise me."

"Oh, yeah. She surprised you, all right."

"Will you listen to..." Griffin's eyes narrowed. "Well, I'll be damned."

"That goes without saying!" Dana slapped her hands on her hips. "There are names for men like you, McKenna. If I weren't such a lady, I'd—"

"I suggest you get down from the pulpit, Anderson." Griffin gripped her shoulders, and swung her towards the lobby door. His voice had gone flat and icy. "You're in no position to give me sermons on morality, considering what just came waltzing in."

Dana's mouth dropped open. "Arthur?" she said, in a choked whisper.

"The Bow Tie, in the flesh." Griffin shook his head. "Hell, lady, I had you pegged all wrong."

"You don't understand. I never..."

"Yeah, I'm sure you didn't, but that's the risk you run, if you play the game. Getting caught is always a possibility." Griffin's hand closed around her wrist. "Time to face the music, babe," he said, and Dana hardly had time to paste a smile on her face before he set off across the lobby, towing her after him.

CHAPTER NINE

GRIFFIN COULDN'T believe it.

The lobby was like a stage set, just before the curtain rises. No action. No sound. Just all the principal characters on their marks, poised and ready to speak their lines in what was rapidly becoming a farce of epic proportions.

There was Cynthia, standing at the desk. And there was the Bow Tie, standing just inside the lobby door.

And here was Dana, bristling with fury.

"Now see what you've done," she said, pulling free of his grasp and hurrying towards Arthur.

Griffin stared after her. What *he* had done? It was such a typically female thing to do, put the blame for this mess on him when he was as innocent as a baby. God knew, he hadn't invited Cynthia to come here. Had Dana invited Arthur? It didn't seem possible, considering the way she'd been kissing him behind the palms a minute ago, but women were unpredictable creatures, yet another reason why they didn't belong in the business world.

"Griffin!"

Griffin pasted a smile to his lips. Cynthia had spotted him. She waved as enthusiastically as a cheerleader at a football game and rushed towards him.

"Cynthia. What a surp—"

"Oh, Griffin," she said, as she flung herself into his arms. It was something she had not done before and something he wished she hadn't done now. He hesitated, then put his arms around her.

Over by the door, the Bow Tie was doing the same thing to Dana.

Bloody hell, Griffin thought bloody *damn* hell!

Cynthia drew back, linked her hands with his, and smiled.

"Are you surprised, darling?"

Surprised? Stunned was a better word. And what was with the "darling" business? Something new had been added.

She laughed gaily. Too gaily, he realized, as her hands turned icy in his.

"I know it's terribly bold of me, and if you want me to leave, you've only to tell me and I'll fly straight home, but I thought—well, Marilyn and I had brunch together, and one word led to another, and she said—"

Griffin felt his blood pressure move up a notch. "My mother suggested this?" he asked, very gently.

"No," Cynthia replied, backtracking quickly, "of course not. We were chatting, that's all, about how some men seem to prefer their women to—to be a tad less conservative in, you know, in their relationships." Color rose in her cheeks. "And I suddenly thought how—how exciting it might be, if I flew down to see you." Her color deepened. "I've done something stupid, Griffin, haven't I? Forgive me. I'll get right into a taxi and—"

"Don't be silly."

"Are you sure?"

There were times in a man's life that a lie was an act of kindness. As for the weekend he'd been anticipating, only moments ago... His gaze focused narrowly on Dana. She was smiling at the Bow Tie and clinging to his arm as if he were Prince Charming.

How could he have ever thought he wanted her in his bed?

"Positive," he said briskly.

Cynthia smiled. "That's wonderful, darling. And I promise, I won't get in the way. I know you have business to transact." Her smile dimmed as she looked past him. "I see I've already taken you away from a meeting. Such an attractive woman. It's hard to imagine she'd be knowledgeable about computer programs."

Griffin looked at the happy couple again. They were deep

in conversation. The Bow Tie's hands rested lightly on Dana's waist, her face was lifted to his in rapt concentration.

"Yes," he said tightly. "It is, isn't it?"

"What does she do?"

Drives me crazy, he thought, and frowned.

"Griffin? Is she here for the conference?"

He nodded. "Actually, she's with Data Bytes. The company I took over. She's the vice president in charge of research and development."

Cynthia's eyes widened. "Really? Oh, I'd like to meet her, Griffin. I always marvel at women who don't mind giving up their femininity to succeed in a man's world," She took his arm and smiled up at him. "Introduce me, darling, would you? Although, perhaps we should wait for a better time. Your vice president does seem to be rather busy, at the moment."

Busy wasn't the word for it. The Bow Tie was playing kissy-face.

"On the other hand," Griffin said, clasping Cynthia's hand, "there's no time like the present."

He reached Dana's side just as her boyfriend was puckering up for another smooch.

"Ms. Anderson," he said with a chill smile, "how nice. I see you've stumbled across an old friend."

Dana's smile was every bit as icy as his. "And so have you, Mr. McKenna. Small world, isn't it?"

"Miniscule." Griffin slipped his arm around Cynthia's waist. "Cynthia Gooding, this is Dana Anderson."

"Delighted, Miss..." Cynthia hesitated. "Haven't we met before?"

"I don't think so," Dana said. It was almost the truth. They hadn't met, officially, they'd simply slipped past each other, in *Portofino*. She held out her hand. Cynthia looked at it, then extended hers. "It's very nice to meet you, Ms. Gooding."

"Oh, please, don't call me Ms." Cynthia laughed gaily and tucked her hand into the crook of Griffin's elbow. "It's Miss. I don't subscribe to all that feminist nonsense, do I, darling?"

Three darlings, or was it four, in just a handful of minutes? A muscle ticked in Griffin's jaw. "No, Cynthia, you do not."

"Well," Dana said briskly, "since I do, why not make it easy on ourselves? I'm Dana, you're Cynthia."

"And I'm Arthur," Arthur said brightly.

"Oh." Dana blushed. "Oh, I'm terribly sorry. Arthur Coakley, this is Griffin McKenna. He's my—"

Arthur laughed. "I know who he is, my dear. Everyone knows Mr. McKenna." He held out his hand. "It's a pleasure."

Griffin nodded as the men shook hands. "How do you do, Coakley?"

"I've followed your career with great interest, Mr. McKenna."

"Griffin," Griffin said. "Or McKenna. Either one. Ms. Anderson never mentioned that she was expecting you."

Arthur chuckled. "She wasn't. I thought I'd surprise her."

"Isn't that lovely?" Cynthia said happily. "I thought I'd surprise Griffin, too."

"An evening filled with surprises," Dana said gaily.

The little group fell silent. After a moment, Griffin spoke.

"Well," he said briskly, "why don't we all have a drink?"

"Lovely," Cynthia said. "But..." She blushed. "I've run into a bit of a problem, darling. At the registration desk. They've just told me there are no rooms. I—I told them...I asked them..." She gave a tinkling laugh. "I said I'd come to spend the weekend with you."

"Isn't that sweet?" Dana's smile could have cut steel.

Griffin smiled back at her. "Sweet," he said, blithely ignoring the fact that his relationship with Cynthia had never progressed beyond a goodnight kiss. "It is, isn't it?"

"...and the clerk was just about to look your name up in the computer, darling, to see what room you were in—"

"Room 2010," Griffin said quickly.

Arthur frowned. "Are you sure? I thought Dana told me that was her room number, when we spoke this afternoon. She said I could call her there, direct, instead of going through the desk.''

"No," Dana said.

"No," Griffin said, at the same instant. He cleared his throat. ''That's the number of the Data Bytes' corporate suite."

Arthur looked even more perplexed. "I don't understand, Dana. Are you and Mr. Mc... Are you and Griffin staying in the same suite?"

"No," Griffin said.

"Yes," Dana said. She gave a trill of laughter as they all turned towards her. "I mean—I mean..."

"She means," Griffin said smoothly, "that we share the parlor room of the suite."

"And that's room 2010?" Arthur shook his head. "I really am confused, Dana. If the parlor is number 2010, then what's the number of your bedroom?"

Dana flashed Griffin a desperate look. "I forget," she said. "Mr. McKenna? Can you—"

"Hell, no." Griffin gave a hearty laugh. "I'm terrible with numbers, Ms. Anderson. You know that." He beamed at Cynthia, who was looking at him with a puzzled expression. "Amazing, isn't it? That a man who's so bad with numbers would be at a computer software conference?"

"It's more than amazing," Arthur said slowly. "I just can't imagine that someone who's made such a killing on Wall Street would be bad with numbers."

"He didn't mean that." All heads turned towards Dana. "I mean...he's bad at remembering simple ones. Unimportant ones. Numbers without dollar signs."

Hell, Griffin thought with disgust, between the two of them, they were digging the hole deeper and deeper.

"I have an idea," he spoke briskly. "Cynthia? Coakley? Have either of you had dinner? Wonderful," he said, before anyone could utter a word. "Ms. Anderson and I were just about to eat. Why don't we continue this conversation in the dining room?"

"All four of us?" Dana said. Her voice came out in a squeak, and she blushed as all eyes fixed on her. "I mean— isn't there some sort of dinner tonight, Mr. McKenna? For conference attendees?"

"We'll skip it."

"But..."

"We'll skip it, Ms. Anderson." Griffin's tone left no room for argument. "Cynthia? Is that all right with you?"

"Why, that would be lovely," Cynthia said. "But first..." Two pink splotches appeared on her cheeks. "The room arrangements, Griffin," she whispered. "So I can have the bell-man put away my luggage..."

"Yes, Mr. McKenna." Dana smiled, but her eyes shot angry sparks. "Do let's discuss the room arrangements."

"Well," Arthur said with a coy smile, "there's no need to fuss. Dana and I..."

"This is a business trip, Coakley."

Griffin spoke coldly. What he really wanted to do was punch the Bow Tie in the nose, but what would that solve? The situation was shaping up pretty clearly. This was the man Dana wanted, the man she loved. And it didn't matter a damn to him. She'd have been a weekend's diversion, nothing more.

"Griffin?" Cynthia gave a nervous little laugh. "Griffin, you're hurting my hand."

He looked down. Cynthia's fingers were trapped within his.

"Oh. I'm sorry, Cynthia. I..."

He let go of her hand and, as he did, his head lifted and his eyes met Dana's. Suddenly, he was back hidden behind the potted palm, with her in his arms. Her face colored. Her breathing quickened. He knew she was remembering the very same thing, and he took a step back.

"Ms. Anderson, why don't you take everyone on through to the dining room while I stop at the desk? I'm sure the clerk will be more than happy to reserve rooms for Cynthia and Arthur at another hotel."

He heard the swift intake of Cynthia's breath. "Oh," she said softly, and turned towards him, so that her back was to the others. "Then—then I'm not going to—to say with you, Griffin?"

His smile tilted. "No, Cynthia," he said gently. He touched her cheek. "I'm sorry, but you're not."

Okay, so McKenna wasn't going to let Cynthia sleep with him.

Well, she wasn't going to let Arthur sleep with her, either. What on earth had gotten into Arthur? Flying down here, without telling her. Making it clear he expected to share her room. Dana frowned. Even if she'd had a room, she wouldn't have let him do that. Their relationship hadn't progressed that far. They'd only known each other a few months.

You know Griffin McKenna a couple of weeks, but you damn well were going to sleep with him, Anderson. If Arthur and Cynthia hadn't shown up...

But they had shown up. And a good thing, too. Sleeping with McKenna would have been the worst mistake of her life. She knew what happened when people who worked together ended up having sex. Their on-the-job relationships fell apart. Why, she could have lost her title...

She could have lost more than that.

No. No, she wouldn't have. Griffin McKenna was exciting, yes. And okay, so she was human. She'd succumbed to his charm, his sexuality...

Almost succumbed. Oh yes. It was a good thing this Cynthia person had come along.

And an even better thing Griffin wasn't going to share his bed with her.

Dana bit her lip. She couldn't have survived that, lying in the darkness through the endless night, knowing that Griffin was making love to another woman, touching her, kissing her, doing all the things he'd been about to do to her.

Would he have slept with Cynthia, if he'd had his own room?

Of course he would have. Cynthia was his—she was his...

What? Not his fiancée. The gossips would have said so. Not

his mistress. There was something too untouchable about her for that.

What was she, then?

Dana peeped over the edge of her oversized menu. Cynthia sat quietly beside her at the dining room table, her menu held just so, her head carefully tilted. She was dressed in a pale peach suit, with tiny pearl studs at her ears and a rope of pearls at her neck. She looked serene and elegant and as perfectly bred as a French poodle.

"So," Dana said brightly, laying her menu on the table, "how long have you known Griff—Mr. McKenna?"

Cynthia looked up and smiled. "Oh, forever. His mother and mine are old friends. Griffin and I went to school together."

"Ah." Dana thought of his silly tale about having worked his way through college. "I'll bet you and he were homecoming king and queen," she said with a false laugh.

"Well..." Cynthia blushed prettily. "I was queen, actually, but by then, Griffin had—left."

"Left?"

"Yes. He went to a different university." She laughed. "Well, a couple of different universities, actually. I don't know the details."

"But you said you went to school together."

"Nursery school. And kindergarten. After that, of course, I attended Miss Livingston's School for Young Ladies, and Griffin went away to board at the Essex Academy. Everyone in our crowd did. You know how it is."

"Of course," Dana said airily, thinking back to the red brick schoolhouse in the middle of Jersey City. "I know how it is."

"And what about your Arthur? Have you known each other long?"

Dana shrugged. "A few months."

Cynthia smiled. "I'll just bet there's a June wedding in the making."

"Well, he hasn't actually asked me to marry him yet..."

"But he will. And, when he does, you'll say 'yes'. It's what every girl wants, isn't it? To have a man take care of her?"

Dana bristled. "I don't need a man to take care of me! No woman does."

"I suppose there are some who feel that way." Cynthia sighed. "I'm afraid I'm quite old-fashioned. So is Griffin. We both agree that a woman should center her life around her husband."

Dana's heartbeat stumbled. That was what Cynthia was, then. Not a lover. Not a mistress. Not even a girlfriend.

Cynthia was the Wife Designate.

"How nice." She forced a smile to her lips. "Then, you should be very happy together."

"Well, as you just said about your young man, Griffin hasn't actually proposed yet, but—"

"But, he will."

"His mother thinks so."

Not just the Wife Designate. Dana's smile wobbled. The Wife Designate, complete with the McKenna Maternal Blessing.

Not that it mattered.

"That's—that's wonderful," she said brightly.

Cynthia sighed. "I just wish—"

"What do you wish?"

Both women looked up. Griffin stood alongside the table. Dana's heart turned over. He was so handsome. So exciting. And he was going to marry Cynthia Gooding, who'd obey his every command, accede to his every wish, bore him to tears for the rest of his life instead of standing up to him, arguing with him, making him so angry that the only way to soothe that anger was to go into his arms...

"What do you wish, Cynthia?" Griffin said again, and Dana leaped to her feet.

"She wishes Arthur would hurry up and come back, so we could get this meal over with." She shot them a wobbly smile, and rushed off in search of Arthur.

In search of sanity.

*   *   *

"They dance well together, don't they, Griffin?"

Griffin's eyes narrowed. Dana and the Bow Tie were waltzing. He'd have laid ten to one odds that the Bow Tie had taken
dancing lessons. Well, Griffin had, too. It was one of the things
you had to do, at Essex, but he'd moved past that silly one,
two, three, thank God. A man could waltz and still manage to
hold a woman close to him, feel her body move against his,
smell her scent.

Cynthia lay her hand on top of his. "Griffin? Don't they
dance well together?"

"Yes," he said, and bared his teeth in what he hoped was
a smile.

"The band's quite good, don't you think?"

He nodded. "Yes," he said again, his eyes riveted to Dana
and the Bow Tie.

"Griffin." Cynthia moved closer. "You haven't danced
with me once this evening."

"Maybe later."

"Just one da—"

"I'm not in the mood, Cynthia."

"Oh."

Griffin sighed. The single word was an accusation that trembled in the air. Hell, he thought glumly, he was being an insensitive bastard, but whose fault was that? Why didn't
Cynthia stand up to him? Why didn't she jab her finger into
his chest and say, listen, McKenna, you are treating me like
dirt and if you don't stop, I'll go someplace where I'm appre-
ciated.

Because she wasn't Dana, that was why.

Dammit, he thought, and turned his back to the dance floor.

"Cynthia."

"Yes?"

Unshed tears glittered in her eyes. Griffin reached out and
cupped her face with his hand.

"Cyn, I'm sorry."

She smiled tremulously.

"You've nothing to apologize for, Griffin."

"I do."

"No. No, you don't."

"Dammit!" Griffin snatched back his hand. "Don't make me out to be a saint when I've been an S.O.B. I know I've been rotten to you, all evening."

"Not all evening. Anyway, you're preoccupied with business. I understand. I never should have dropped in on you." She smiled again, but one perfect tear rolled down her cheek. "I just wanted to do something that would surprise you."

He sighed and blotted the tear with his fingertip. "Yeah, well, you certainly did that."

Cynthia looked towards the dance floor. "She's very pretty, your Miss Anderson."

"Is she? I hadn't really—"

"Smart, too. She has strange ideas, though. She's one of those feminists."

"She's very independent, Cynthia."

"Did you see how she took over? Pulling out her chair without waiting for Arthur to do it, telling the waiter what she wanted to eat instead of letting Arthur do it for her." Cynthia shook her head. "I never saw such a thing."

"Well, the Bow...Coakley should have said something, if he didn't like it."

"A man shouldn't have to say something. A woman should be feminine and wait for the man to make certain decisions."

"Dana is feminine."

"Well, I suppose she looks feminine enough, though, actually, that outfit is—well, it's—"

"Yes?"

"Obvious, you know? That slit in the skirt. That neckline. I'm sure her beau would prefer her to dress in a more discrete fashion."

Griffin looked across the dance floor. The band had segued into a tango. The Bow Tie was dipping Dana back over his arm. Her hair trailed out behind her, like a golden flame; her out thrust leg was exposed from ankle to thigh.

"She looks..." He cleared his throat. "She looks all right."

The music changed yet again, became soft and dreamy. The lights dimmed. The Bow Tie tried to draw Dana closer but she didn't seem cooperative. Then her eyes met Griffin's. Her chin lifted, and she melted into the Bow Tie's embrace.

Griffin's vision clouded.

The Bow Tie's hands slid down Dana's back and settled at the base of her spine. Dana slid her arms around his neck.

"Enough," Griffin snarled, and shot to his feet.

"Griffin? Darling, what is it?"

"It's late," he said, dumping bills on the table. "Tomorrow's a long day."

"I haven't finished my—" Cynthia blinked as Griffin dragged back her chair, pulled her to her feet and hurried her across the dance floor. "Griffin." She gave a little laugh. "If you'd just slow down…"

Dana and the Bow Tie were swaying to the music. Dana's head was on his shoulder; her eyes were closed. Griffin muttered something under his breath and tapped her on the shoulder.

"Time to call it a night, Anderson."

She lifted her head and stared at him. "I beg your pardon?"

"I said, it's late, and we have to get an early start in the morning."

"But—"

"Coakley?"

He thought, just for a minute, that Coakley was going to protest. Something masculine and primitive stirred deep inside him. Come on, he thought, and almost smiled, come on, man, just give me an excuse…

"Yes," Arthur said. He let go of Dana and his bow tie slid up, then down, as he swallowed. "Dana, Mr. Mc—I mean, Griffin is right. We've all had a long day."

Griffin took Dana's elbow. "Indeed," he said, and strode from the nightclub with one woman on each arm.

Dana spun towards him as soon as they reached the lobby.

"Let go of me, McKenna!"

"I told you, it's late."

"I am your employee, not your property. When I decide it's time to call it a night, I'll—"

"You should have done that hours ago. You have to finish working on that code, Anderson, or have you forgotten your responsibilities?"

"I told you, I'm almost done with the code. Another half an hour—"

"Well, I want that half an hour put in tonight, not tomorrow morning."

Dana took a step back. "You are, without a doubt, the most selfish son of a—"

"Griffin!" Cynthia's face was white. "Are you going to let her talk to you that way?"

"Now, Griffin." Arthur's face was even whiter. "Surely, you can speak a little more politely."

"Stay out of this, Coakley."

"Yes, Arthur." Dana's eyes flashed. "Stay out of this. This is between Simon Legree and me."

Griffin let go of Cynthia and moved towards Dana. "Go to your room," he said in a soft, cold voice.

"I am not a child, McKenna!"

"You are an employee, and this is not a vacation. If you want to keep your job, you'll do as you're told."

"My room?" Dana's voice shook with rage. "*My* room? Don't you mean that travesty they call the br—"

Oh God. The Bridal Suite, she'd almost said, and then she'd have lost everything. Her job. Her promotion. Arthur's respect, because he'd never believe the truth. Who would? Not even Cynthia, the limpet, who just stood there with her silly mouth open and her hands pressed to her cheeks, would believe the truth, that she and the Mighty McKenna were sharing the Bridal Suite when the only thing they should have been sharing was ten rounds in a boxing ring.

"I hate you, McKenna," she whispered shakily.

"Oh, Dana." Arthur was almost moaning with anguish. "Mr. McKenna. She doesn't mean—"

"She does," Griffin said coldly, "and that's fine, Coakley.

I demand results from my employees, not affection. And now, if you and Cynthia will come with me, I'll have the doorman call a cab.''

"Dana?" Arthur said. He licked his lips. "Dana, shall I leave?"

Dana jerked her chin up. "If you have to ask such a question, Arthur, you don't need me to give you an answer."

She turned on her heel, marched across the lobby and into the waiting elevator, holding back her angry tears until the doors slid shut on the sight of Griffin McKenna clasping both his charges by the arms as he herded them to the door.

CHAPTER TEN

DANA rammed her electronic key-card into the lock on the door of the Bridal Suite. The little light in the panel blinked green and she pushed the door open, then slammed it shut.

"McKenna," she said, flinging the key-card across the empty room, "you are a first-class, dirty, rotten skunk!"

Her shoes went sailing after the key-card...shoes McKenna had chosen, shoes no sensible woman would have gone near except in a teenage boy's fevered dreams. Skinny straps, skinny, spike heels... Walking in shoes like that could become an Olympic event. Sexist stilts, she thought coldly, just the sort of thing a man like McKenna would like.

The nerve of him.

"The nerve," Dana said, storming into the bathroom, peeling off the ivory silk suit and drop-kicking it into the corner. Ordering her around. Telling her what to do. Telling *everybody* what to do! Buying her an outrageous outfit, buying her underwear—*underwear,* for heaven's sake, and then asking if she were wearing it.

Of course, she'd worn it. What else could she do? She couldn't have worn her own things under the ivory silk, not when the top was cut down to her whatsis and the skirt was cut up to her whosis...

...*Not when she could close her eyes and imagine McKenna seeing her in it.*

Dana snatched one of the terry-cloth robes from its hook and put it on.

What a ridiculous thought! She'd sooner find herself the love object of a baboon! McKenna had been right about one thing, anyway. It had, indeed, been a long day. What she needed now was a good night's sleep, and to hell with his ordering her to get to work on the code tonight. What did he know about codes and programming, anyway?

"Nothing," she muttered as she marched through the living room again. Not one miserable thing. So far as she could tell, the only thing Griffin McKenna knew was how to run a dictatorship.

Dana opened the sliding-glass doors that led onto the terrace. The air was warm, rich with the scent of the ocean that foamed against the shore below. She sighed, leaned her elbows on the terrace railing and gazed out over the dark water.

Such a sweet thing Arthur had done, flying down to join her. She'd never have imagined him doing something so impulsive.

"What ever possessed you?" she'd asked him as they'd danced, and Arthur had blushed and replied that he'd just wanted to surprise her.

"You see?" he'd said with a little smile. "I'm not always a cautious stick-in-the-mud."

The evening had been so nice, until McKenna had—

Oh, hell.

Dana turned her back to the night, sank down into a wicker chair and rubbed her hands over her eyes.

Why kid herself? The evening had been horrible, from the minute she'd spotted Arthur in the lobby, straight through to when McKenna had sent her packing.

What a farce! Pretending it was fun to watch Arthur damn near clicking his heels and saluting each time McKenna opened his mouth.

"Yes, Griffin." Dana dropped her chin, and her voice, to her chest. "Whatever wine you prefer is fine, Griffin. You're going to have the red snapper? Well, then, I'll have it, too."

Cynthia's performance had been even worse. The little-girl voice. The demure looks. The way she'd hung on McKenna's every pronouncement as if he were giving the Sermon on the Mount.

Not that he'd said much. What he'd done most was glower. That was why, when Cynthia had nervously suggested it might be fun to peek into the hotel's nightclub, Dana had jumped at the chance.

Anything, she'd figured, was better than sitting around like a bunch of mourners at a wake.

"Let's," she'd said quickly, before Griffin could frown and cast his royal veto.

But when not even the noise and the music in the small, artificially darkened room had been enough to lift the gloom, Dana had grabbed Arthur's hand and said she wanted to dance.

"Dance?" Arthur had replied as if she'd suggested they go parasailing over the Atlantic.

"Dance," she'd said firmly. "Remember those lessons you told me about? Why let them go to waste?"

It had been an argument Arthur could not resist. He'd followed her onto the stamp-size dance floor, where she'd practically had to beg him to put his arms around her.

"I already have them around you," he'd insisted.

It was an accurate assessment, by his reckoning. His right arm encircled her waist, hand planted neatly in the middle of her back. His left arm was upraised, elbow out, so that his hand could hold hers. A chaperone at a high school prom would have applauded, but Dana wanted something else.

"Hold me as if you meant it," she'd said, trying not to make it sound like a command. "Look around you at other people, Arthur. See what I mean?"

He looked, he saw, but he went on leading her around the floor with enough space between them to have parked a bus. In the end, she'd resorted to a pure, unadulterated lie.

"I want you to hold me close," she'd whispered, batting her lashes.

Dana groaned at the memory.

Oh, what a rotten thing to have done! She hadn't wanted Arthur to hold her at all. She'd wanted to drive McKenna crazy.

And she'd succeeded.

Her pulse quickened at the memory of Griffin's face once Arthur's arms had finally enfolded her. The narrowed eyes.

The flared nostrils. She'd read a description once, of a stallion preparing to defend his mares against an interloper...

In another time, another place, she knew he'd have come for her, torn her from Arthur's embrace, carried her off to his castle and made passionate love to her until she pleaded for mercy, until she clung to him and whispered the truth, that she wanted him, that she'd never stop wanting him.

Dana bowed her head. She sat still for a long moment. Then, slowly, she rose to her feet.

She was tired. That was why she was thinking these wild thoughts. What she needed was a good night's rest, without sight or sound or thought of Griffin McKenna, and there was only one way to guarantee that.

Resolutely, she marched to the door of the Bridal Suite and pulled the Do Not Disturb sign from the knob. Let him sleep in the lobby. Let him sleep on the beach. Let him curl up outside the door, like the cur he was.

The one place he was not going to sleep, was here.

She felt a weight lift from her shoulders. Of course, he wasn't going to sleep here. Why hadn't she put her foot down when this craziness all began? He could take a room at another hotel. So what if he had to gallop back and forth once the conference began?

Dana's chin rose as she opened the door. She was the programmer, not Griffin. He might like to think he had to be available every minute of every hour, but the simple truth was that she was the indispensable one, this weekend, not—

The elevator doors whooshed open. Griffin stepped into the corridor.

"Dana?"

She froze, but only for an instant.

"Griffin," she said politely, and then she looped the Do Not Disturb sign over the knob, slipped inside, and slammed the door.

His footsteps pounded down the corridor.

Safe inside, she fumbled for the security chain. She heard the swish of his key-card in the lock, but she was quicker. The chain fell into place and, triumphantly, she pushed the door closed.

"Dana." The doorknob rattled. "Open this door."

"No." She shook her head and flattened her palms against the door. "I'm not opening it."

"Don't be an idiot. Open the door."

"That's how you've been treating me, as if I were an idiot." She drew a shuddering breath. "Well, I'm through letting you get away with it, McKenna. You think you can boss people around, have your own way all the time—"

"Open the door, Anderson."

Dana shut her eyes. Oh, that voice. She could just imagine the face that went with it, the burning eyes, the thinned mouth...

"Anderson!" Griffin's fist slammed against the door. "Do you hear me? Open it, I said."

"Try hearing me for a change," she said. "I loathe you. I hate you. I despise you. Am I getting through to you, McKenna?"

"Anderson. If you want to keep your job—"

"You can't fire me. Not now, anyway. You need me to debug that program."

"I'm going to count to ten. And then you'd better open this damned door because if you don't—"

"I'm not listening," she said, and turned the lock. "Go away."

"Look, I don't know what you're so ticked off about, but—"

"That's exactly the point. You don't know. You should, but you don't."

He sighed. With her ear to the door, she could hear it as clearly as if he were in the room with her.

"Is this about my suggesting Cynthia and the Bow—and Coakley leave, so we could call it a night?"

"Suggesting?" She stepped back and folded her arms. "Suggesting?" she said, and gave a little laugh.

"Okay. Okay, maybe I was a little abrupt—"

"It's too late for apologies. You're a horrible person, Griffin McKenna, and I hate you."

"You already said that."

"I despise you."

"That, too."

"Well, it's worth saying again."

Griffin shut his eyes and leaned his forehead against the door. "Dana, for God's sake, be reasonable. Where am I going to sleep?"

"What do I care? Sleep on the beach. Sleep in a telephone booth. Sleep with Cynthia." Her voice quavered, though there was no reason for it. "Why miss a night, if you don't have to?"

"I don't sleep with—" He heard a door crack open somewhere behind him. Oh, hell, he thought miserably. "I don't sleep with Cynthia," he said in a low voice. "Not that it's any of your business."

"You're right. It's absolutely none of my business. Why don't you?"

How many times had he asked himself that same question? "What kind of question is that? I don't know why I don't sleep with her. Why don't you sleep with the Bow Tie?"

"How do you know I don't?"

"I just do," he said, and wondered why he felt so damned relieved. "Why don't you?"

Why, indeed? "Our relationship's on a higher plane than that."

"Well, I'm delighted for you both, but I still need a place to bunk for the night."

"Try the lobby. Some of those chairs looked pretty comfortable."

Another door creaked open down the hall.

"Anderson." Griffin did his best to sound like the very voice of reason. "Let me in."

"I don't want to."

"Dammit, Anderson, I'm telling you for the last time—"

"What's the problem, young man?"

Griffin stepped away from the door and looked around. A woman was peering out from behind the door of her hotel room. She had curlers in her hair and a look of perplexity on her face.

"Problem?" he said.

"Yes. Why are you talking to that door?"

"I, ah, I'm not. I'm talking to, ah, to—"

"What does it say there?" The woman peered nearsightedly at the brass plaque on the door of Room 2010. "Brindle Suit? What's a brindle suit?"

Griffin cleared his throat. "No. I mean, it says—it says—" He gestured helplessly. "I'm sorry we disturbed you, madam. Why don't you just—"

"Ah, I can make it out now." The woman's wispy brows lifted. "It says Bridal Suite."

"Yes. Yes, it does. Look, just go on back to bed. I apologize if—"

"My, oh, my, did you forget your key? Are you locked out?"

Oh Lord, Griffin thought, why me? "Madam, really, I appreciate your concern, but really—"

"You just wait there, young man. I'll phone the desk and have them send someone up to open that door for you."

"No," Griffin said...and then he cocked his head. "Why, yes. Yes, thank you, madam. If you'd just wait a second, while I tell my—bride—the good news... Darling?" He leaned closer to the door. "Dana, dearest? Did you hear that? One of our neighbors has offered to call the desk. They'll send someone up to open the door."

"No one's going to open this door, McKenna. I've got the chain on, remember?"

Griffin sighed. "You say the chain is stuck? Well, I'll tell our Good Samaritan to have the desk send up a maintenance crew. They can take the door off the hinges." He folded his arms and stared at the door, his face a study in concern. "That should draw quite a crowd."

A second passed. The chain rattled free, the lock turned and the door swung open. Griffin looked at the woman with the curlers in her hair.

"Isn't that remarkable? My bride's managed to open the door, all by herself."

She smiled. "Sweet dreams, young man."

"The same to you, madam," Griffin said, and stepped inside the Bridal Suite. The door slammed shut, and he came face-to-face with Dana.

"The only thing more horrendous than spending the night in the same suite as you," she said, "would be having everyone on this floor *know* that I was spending the night in the same suite as you."

Griffin's jaw tightened. He'd never been so angry at a woman in his life. It seemed impossible to think that this—this undersize wraith in an oversize robe had kept him cooling his heels in a hotel corridor. He could have pushed her over with one finger, if he'd been into pushing women, and, dammit, he wanted to do exactly that. Hell, he thought, jamming his hands into his pockets, he most certainly wanted to do exactly that!

"For once," he said, "we agree. You ever try and make a public spectacle of me again, you'll pay the price."

"Oh, give me a break, McKenna! If there's anybody into making public spectacles of people, it's you!"

"I beg your pardon," he said coldly.

"Bossing me around. Telling me to go to my room, as if I were a ten-year-old!"

"You have a job to do, in case you've forgotten." He stalked past her, yanked off his jacket and tossed it on a chair. "I know you'd rather pretend this is a holiday weekend, that the only thing you've got to do is—is climb all over that boyfriend of yours on a public dance floor, but—"

"I was not climbing all over anybody!" Dana skidded around Griffin and stopped in front of him, her hands on her hips.

"No?"

"No."

"Did you finish working on that code?"

"Are you kidding? I just got up here. I haven't even had time to take off my makeup."

But she'd had time to get undressed. The long robe kept gaping open. Not even the slit in the skirt of the ivory silk suit had showed as much long, luscious leg as the robe was showing now.

Griffin felt a sudden tightening in his groin.

"Get out of my way," he growled.

"First, we talk. Then, I'll be happy to oblige!"

Did she have to do that? Tilt back her head, so that her hair slid down over her shoulders?

"Dammit," he said through his teeth, "step aside!"

"I have no wish to see your face or hear your voice, McKenna."

"Amen to that. Now, get out of—"

"As for the code, I'll be up at dawn to work on it."

He pulled off his tie and tossed it after the jacket. "I expect as much."

"Now that that's settled, I'm going to bed." She glared at him. "And I promise you, I'm going to take your advice and bolt my door."

"Why?"

"Why? What do you mean, why? Because..." She hesitated. He was undoing his shirt, peeling it off his shoulders, and dropping it to the floor. "What are you doing, McKenna?"

"I'm getting undressed."

"Well, stop." She swallowed, glared, snatched up his shirt and held it out. "Would you please put this on?"

He looked at the shirt, then at her. "What for? I'm getting ready for bed. I don't sleep in my clothes, Anderson. Do you?"

"No. Of course not. I mean..." What did she mean? She couldn't think, not with him standing around shirtless. Such golden skin. Such beautiful muscles. And that curling dark hair, stretching over his chest, down his flat, taut belly, into the waistband of his trousers...

"What do you sleep in, then?"

Her gaze flew upward. He was looking at her, his eyes dark and heavy-lidded.

"That's a ridiculous question."

"Is it?"

Those eyes. So dark. And so focused. So tightly fixed on her...

"Why are you so angry at me, Anderson?"

His voice was soft, caressing. She felt a flutter along her spine.

"You know why. You treated me like—like a slave. 'Anderson, do this. Do that...'"

"You were all over him on that dance floor."

Dana colored. "I wasn't!"

"He's in love with you, the poor bastard." Griffin moved toward her, his steps slow and deliberate, his eyes never leaving hers. "But you're not in love with him."

"Don't be silly. You don't know anything about... What are you doing?"

His smile was slow, dangerous, and heart-stoppingly sexy. "You never did answer my question, Anderson." He reached out and took hold of the sash on the robe. "Did you wear the lingerie I sent up?"

"I told you I didn't. McKenna, what are you...?"

"I want to see for myself."

Dana's heart thumped crazily. He was undoing the sash, letting the ends slip through his fingers.

"Are you calling me a liar?" she said unsteadily.

"Are you asking me not to do this?" he said just as unsteadily.

Time seemed to stop. The robe fell open, but Griffin's eyes remained locked on hers.

"Dana," he said, his voice a husky whisper.

"Yes," she said, "oh, yes..."

And then she was in his arms.

She had expected him to undress her, there in the living room.

He didn't. He swept her up into his arms, carried her swiftly through the suite to the bedroom, where the soft light of the moon teased the darkness.

He kissed her then, with a hot, sweet abandon that made her heart pound.

Slowly, so slowly that it seemed to take an eternity, he lowered her down his body, until her feet touched the floor.

"Let me see you," he said, and she held her breath as he drew the robe back from her shoulders.

Her heart thudded even harder as he looked at her. She had never had a man look at her this way before. Not touching, not stroking, but touching and stroking just the same, with his gaze. She felt her breasts swell, her nipples harden.

"Beautiful," he whispered, and she knew that she was, if only for this night. If only for this man.

The robe slipped to the carpet. He looked at her for a long moment, his face barred by moonlight, and then he reached out, undid the laces on the camisole, and drew it from her.

His breath caught. She saw his features grow taut with desire.

"My beautiful Dana."

He knelt before her, drew off the wisp of lace that were her panties. His hands lingered on her skin, caressing her, touching her, until she cried out his name. Then he leaned forward, his breath fanning her thighs, and put his mouth on her.

The shock of the kiss sent a white-hot lick of flame through her blood. She felt herself shatter and she cried out, half in passion, half in disbelief. No, she thought, no, it couldn't end so quickly. She wanted what was about to happen to last forever.

He kissed her again. A sob burst from her throat. She swayed, clutched at his shoulders for support.

"No," she sobbed. "Griffin, please..."

"Yes," he said fiercely, and he caught her up in his arms again and carried her to the bed. Down, spiraling down in want and need, she tumbled into the softness of the silk sheets.

She watched as he undressed. How beautiful he was. The broad shoulders, the ridged chest and belly. The narrow hips and long, muscled legs...

And the part of him that was pure, unadulterated male.

He came down to her, and she went into his arms, opening her mouth for his kisses, lifting herself to him so that he could taste her breasts, lick her belly, inhale her scent as she was inhaling his.

"Griffin," she whispered, "I want...I want..."

"Everything," he said, and entered her on one long, deep, heart-wrenching thrust.

She came apart instantly, shattering like crystal even as he sheathed himself in her heat, and her last thought, before she could think no more, was that if hating Griffin McKenna was like this, what would happen when she admitted that she loved him?

Griffin awoke hours later with Dana still asleep in his arms.

She lay on her side, turned toward him, her head nestled against his shoulder, her mouth inches from his throat. Each soft breath she took sent a whisper of warmth along his skin.

It was late. Very late. The moon had slipped across the sky, submerging the bedroom in the velvet darkness of the night.

Griffin shifted his weight just a little. Dana sighed, and nestled closer. Her hair, soft as silk, brushed against his lips. He tilted his head and buried his nose in her hair. It smelled of flowers. Lilies? Lilacs? He wasn't very good with flowers. The only ones he knew by sight were roses. Long-stemmed, hot-house roses, the kind he'd sent, over the years, to dozens of women.

He smiled. Somehow, he didn't think the woman in his arms would be impressed by hothouse roses. Griffin drew her closer. Wasn't there something called a desert rose? If there wasn't, there ought to be. A rose—perfect, sweet-smelling, beautiful...and surrounded by prickly thorns.

Dana murmured in her sleep. Griffin put his hand against her cheek, stroked the pad of his thumb over her silky skin.

"What is it, love?" he whispered.

She sighed, and his name slipped from her lips. She was dreaming, and of him.

A feeling like none he'd ever felt before seemed to expand inside his chest.

Of him, he thought, and he rolled onto his side, gathered her tightly into his embrace, and let the warmth of her, the feel of her, draw him down into deep, deep sleep.

When he awoke again, it was morning.

Bright sunlight streamed across the room. Griffin groaned a protest, reached out for Dana...

But he was alone in the bed. If he hadn't known otherwise, he'd have thought he'd been alone all night. There wasn't a sign of her. The covers had been smoothed back where she'd lain, the pillows plumped.

He sat up and ran his hands through his hair. He was the one who usually made an early retreat. Not that he ran out, right after making love. Women liked to be held. He knew that. He even liked to hold them, to make that feeling of completeness that came after good sex last just a little while longer. So, he stayed in a woman's bed for a while. Half an hour, an hour—once in a very great while, he stayed until early morning.

He didn't believe in one-night stands. He always phoned the next day, sent flowers, whatever, suggested dinner and the theater and kept things going for a civilized stretch of time, until he lost interest, which he invariably did...

Griffin frowned and swung his feet to the floor.

Where the hell was Dana?

He pulled on his trousers, zipped the fly, and strode from the bedroom.

"Dana?"

He stopped halfway through the living room. She was out on the terrace; he could see her clearly through the glass, sitting cross-legged on the chaise with her portable computer in her lap. That she'd gone to work straight from bed was obvious: she was wearing the terry-cloth robe, she'd pulled her hair into a curly tumble on top of her head, and her face was scrubbed and shiny-clean.

Griffin felt as if a hand had closed around his heart.

She was so beautiful.

He must have made a sound because suddenly she looked up and saw him. Her eyes lit; pink swept into her cheeks and she lifted her hand to her hair in a gesture so feminine, so unaware, that it made his throat constrict.

She smiled, and mouthed ''hello.''

He smiled, and mouthed it back, when what he really wanted to do was go to her, take her in his arms, tell her—tell her...

She tapped the keyboard, then rose, the computer tucked under one arm, and slid open the terrace door.

''Hi,'' she said.

''Hi.''

''I've got good news.''

He nodded. Her feet were bare, her toenails unpolished. He couldn't recall seeing a woman's toenails without polish before.

''Griffin?''

He looked at her face. Her beautiful face. She was smiling.

''I solved the problem with the code.''

''Ah.'' Slowly, he started toward her. ''That's great.''

''It just took a little... Griffin? What are you doing?''

Gently, he took the computer from her hands and put it on the table.

''Griffin?'' she said, her voice suddenly husky. ''Don't you want to hear about the code?''

He nodded, his face solemn. ''I want to hear all about it,'' he said as he undid the belt of her robe. ''Every last detail.''

Her head fell back as he bent and kissed her breasts. She moaned, and clasped his head.

''Griffin...Griffin, I can't—I can't think if you—if you...''

He swung her up into his arms. She lifted her face for his kiss, and he carried her through the Bridal Suite, back to bed.

CHAPTER ELEVEN

GUILT.

That was what Dana felt. Guilt, as drowning-deep as the ocean that beat against the shore below, as hot and suffocating as the heat of the late morning.

She stood on the terrace of the Bridal Suite, her hands clutching the railing, and tried to convince herself that she had nothing to feel guilty about.

She was not committed to anyone. Neither was Griffin. They were adults, and unencumbered. What they had done could hurt nobody.

Her fingers curled more tightly around the railing.

Who was she kidding? There were two people in a hotel moments from here who'd be devastated if they knew that she and Griffin had made love. Arthur had flown all this distance to be with her. He was in love with her, and she knew it. Just because he'd never said it didn't make it less true.

And Cynthia. Cynthia, who looked at Griffin with her heart glowing in her eyes...

"Sweetheart?"

Dana closed her eyes at the sound of Griffin's voice. She heard the terrace doors slide open, then felt his body brush lightly against her.

His arms went around her, and he drew her back against him.

Don't, she told herself. Oh, don't. This is wrong. It's wrong...

"Dana."

He put his mouth to her throat, and her breath caught. I love you, she thought, oh, Griffin, I love you. What was the sense in trying to deny it?

But he didn't love her. This was a weekend's amusement for him, and that made what they'd done even worse. To deceive two perfectly nice people, just so she could lie in the arms of a man who would never whisper those magic words...

"Where'd you go? I woke up and you were gone." He nuzzled her hair aside and lightly nipped the tender skin just behind her ear. "I missed you."

"I—I felt restless."

"Restless?" He laughed softly and turned her toward him. Her throat tightened at the sight of him—his tousled hair, his sexy, unshaven face. "I've got a cure for that," he said, tilting her face up to his. "All you had to do was wake me."

"Griffin." Dana put her hands on his chest. "Griffin, I've been thinking..."

"So have I."

He smiled and sought her mouth, but she turned her face away.

"Please. Listen to me." She took a deep breath. "I—I was thinking about—about Arthur."

"Thinking about what?" His smile tilted. "You're not accountable to him."

"I know. And you don't owe anything to Cynthia. But—"

Griffin lay his index finger against her lips.

"We didn't ask them to fly here, Dana."

"No, of course not. Still—"

"And we didn't plan what happened to us."

She smiled. It was so ridiculous, even to suggest such a thing.

"You're right, we didn't." She laughed softly. "Actually, if I'd thought about us being together, I'd have bet on one of us tossing the other into the Atlantic."

"Into the Atlantic, huh?" Griffin chuckled. "If I'd known my new V.P. was entertaining murderous thoughts, I'd never have agreed to share a suite with her."

Dana's smile faded. "We shouldn't have agreed to share it, Griffin. If we hadn't—"

Griffin bent his head and kissed her. She tried to hold back, but how could she, when his mouth was so sweet? She groaned, lifted her arms and put them around his neck.

"We could have stayed on two different floors," he whispered, "and it wouldn't have mattered. This was inevitable, Dana. You must feel that, the same as I do."

She nodded, and leaned her forehead against his chin.

"I do. But I keep thinking about Arthur. And—"

"I know a way to solve that problem," Griffin said as he swung her into his arms and carried her inside.

"No." Dana put her hand gently over his lips. "We have to go downstairs. The presentations are going to begin soon. The demo—"

"To hell with the demo."

"You don't mean that."

He sighed. She was right. Data Bytes was in a precarious state, and close to collapse. But, as he lowered her gently to the floor, it occurred to him that it was his heart that should be worrying him.

All of a sudden, it felt as fragile as glass.

The computer software section of the conference hall was crowded with representatives from more than a dozen companies, but most of the crowd had gathered around the Data Bytes exhibit.

The program demo wasn't just up and running, it was running perfectly. Griffin couldn't remember the last time he'd shaken so many hands and accepted so many congratulations.

"Don't pat me on the back," he kept saying. "The program's the brainchild of my Vice President, Dana Anderson."

At last, the crowd thinned. Griffin pretended to heave a sigh of relief. "We made it," he said, "Thanks to you."

"Agreed." Dana grinned and wrinkled her nose at him. "But you're the reason the program is selling. Much as it pains me to admit it, you were right. You're the guy everybody wants to meet."

"I think we should go somewhere and celebrate." He took

her hand in his and played with her fingers. "How about lunch?"

"Lunch." Dana sighed. "Good idea."

"Lobster salad and a bottle of chilled white wine?"

"Umm. Even better."

"Good." He moved closer and smiled into her eyes. "We can order in."

"Order in?"

"We'll have it upstairs, in our suite." His fingers laced through hers. "Lunch—and a long, relaxing soak in that tub. How's that sound?"

Dana flushed. There was no mistaking his meaning. "Now?"

Griffin gave a low, sexy laugh. "Right now."

"But isn't there some sort of speech in half an... Griffin. Don't look at me that way."

"Come upstairs with me, Dana. Let me get you out of that dress, take your hair down and—"

"McKenna? Hey, man, great program."

Griffin looked up. A guy he'd gone to school with, the rep from a major Boston banking conglomerate, was beaming at him. For one wild minute, he thought of telling him that his timing was lousy, but Dana had already discreetly disengaged her hand from his and moved away. So he sighed, did his best to look pleased, and stuck out his hand.

"Evans," he said. "Nice to see you again."

"Same here. You know, I read about you buying up this company, but I had no idea you'd..."

Evans droned on. Griffin tried to pay attention. He smiled, nodded, managed an occasional, "Is that so?" but his thoughts weren't on the conversation, they were on Dana.

She was standing a couple of feet away, explaining the program to some guy who obviously didn't know the difference between a computer chip and a potato chip. Griffin's eyes narrowed. It didn't take much to see that they guy's interest was less on the program and more on Dana, but she kept demonstrating the program, pointing out its strengths with such care that, after a while, the guy began to focus on the monitor. At last, you could almost see the lightbulb going on over his head.

"I get it," he said, and Dana smiled in a way that had to make him feel as if he'd won an Olympic gold medal.

The guy said something. Dana smiled again, and they shook hands. Griffin relaxed. Amazing. The guy had gone from seeing her as an object of desire to accepting her as an intelligent human being. It wasn't an easy transition for most men, himself included. The truth was that she was right. Nobody wanted to admit that it was still pretty much a man's world.

God, she was wonderful. He'd never known anyone like her. The hardest thing he'd ever done, in his life, was to let her leave his arms this morning and come down here, where he had to share her with a couple of hundred people. How long would it be before he'd be alone with her again?

"...Fair warning, McKenna."

Griffin tuned in just in time to see Evans give him a wink.

"I'm dead serious, you know."

"Uh, I'm sorry, Tim. I must have missed something. Fair warning about what?"

"About hiring away that Veep of yours. She ever wants to make a move to Massachusetts, all she's got to do is say so. Brains and beauty, McKenna. That's one hell of a combination."

"Yes. Yes, I suppose it is."

"We can use a gal like that in our company."

"A woman like that," Griffin said easily.

Evans punched him lightly in the arm. "Will wonders never cease? Affirmative action's finally gotten to you, has it?"

"Have to keep up with the times," Griffin said, smiling as the men shook hands. "And, Evans—don't hold your breath. Dana Anderson isn't about to leave Data Bytes."

She sure as hell wasn't, he thought as Evans strolled away. Not for Boston, or anywhere else that would take her away from New York, and from him. Griffin folded his arms, leaned back against the display table and watched as she explained the new program to yet another interested conference attendee. No way, he thought. He'd found himself a miracle, and he was going to hold on to it.

He watched as she fielded a tough question about the new program with a dazzling combination of charm and reason. Evans was right. Beauty and brains, all in one package. Her hair was loose today, a concession he'd won only after telling her, straight-faced, that if she pinned it back, he'd take it down right in the conference hall. She was wearing a butter-yellow dress, very simple and proper, but feminine and pretty, too. She'd ordered some things by telephone from the little shop where he'd bought the ivory silk suit last night. To his relief, her request for "something businesslike" had led not to the shapeless stuff he'd always seen on her until now. Instead, the shop had sent up two dresses, this yellow one and another in pale violet.

Griffin had watched her place the order just a few hours ago.

"I'll need two outfits," she'd said crisply. "Simple lines, no frills, something suitable for business, in size eight."

Her tone had been the only no-nonsense thing about her, considering that she'd made the call while she was sitting cross-legged in the center of their rumpled bed, wearing nothing but one of his shirts, with him sitting just behind her.

"And a dress to wear tonight," he'd whispered, kissing her temple.

"I don't need a dress for tonight," she'd whispered back. "There's that dinner, and a guest speaker..."

"Something black and slinky," he'd said, slipping his hand inside her shirt.

"Griffin," she'd said breathlessly, clapping her hand over the phone, "I can't—you have to stop..."

And he had stopped, after she'd ordered something black and silky, and then he'd taken the phone from her hand and tumbled her back onto the sheets.

"Stop what?" he'd murmured, and then she was in his arms again and he was on fire...

Griffin frowned, shifted his weight, and told himself to think about something else before he became a public embarrassment.

Think about tonight, and the dinner reservations he'd made at a little place on the water the concierge had told him about. Think about later, when they got back to their suite and the door closed behind them. Think about...

Oh, hell.

Think about Cynthia and Arthur, who'd just come through the door at the far end of the room.

Somehow, he'd managed not to think about them after he'd called Cynthia at her hotel, shrugged off a guilty twinge at the sound of her voice, and explained he'd be tied up most of the day.

"That's all right," she'd said. "I understand."

No, he'd wanted to tell her, no, you don't understand...but in the end, he hadn't because he didn't understand, either. Something was happening to him, and he knew it, something that was as terrifying as it was exhilarating. He was feeling an emotion he couldn't quite identify, one he wasn't ready to examine too closely but one he wasn't about to walk away from, either.

One thing was certain. He had to tell Cynthia that they had no future together. He'd known it , and he'd done his best to let her see it, but either he'd been too subtle or she hadn't been listening, or maybe, if he took a good, hard look at himself and was brutally honest, maybe he'd been content to let her stand around while he toyed with the possibility that someday he might care enough to want to marry her.

He wouldn't. He knew that now. Cynthia was a nice woman, with a good heart, but she wasn't the woman for him and she never would be. If he married, it would be for love. That was something else he'd finally figured out. His father had married the same way he'd done business, the same way he'd raised his son. Coldly, expediently, measuring what he'd invested in his relationships against what he'd expected to gain. With an attitude like that, he'd gotten exactly what he'd deserved.

Griffin supposed he'd always known that was the wrong way to go about marriage, but it had taken a feisty computer programmer with a defiant tilt to her chin to make him acknowledge it. Marriage had nothing to do with expediency and everything to do with love, and love had nothing to do with gain and everything to do with the loss of yourself in another person.

When a man took a wife, it ought to be because he'd found the one woman who could enrich his life, bring him passion and joy, share his interests, and his dreams.

His dreams? What about the Bow Tie's dreams? Wasn't that why Coakley had flown down here, because he was in love with Dana and wanted to marry her?

Griffin's heart pounded. He had to do something, fast. He had to grab hold of Dana, tell her that—tell her that—that *if* he ever fell in love, *if* he ever decided to marry—

"Griffin?"

Dana turned toward him. Her face was white. She'd spotted Cynthia and Arthur.

"Dana." He took her hand. It was icy cold. "Sweetheart, listen to me—"

"Griffin. I can't face them! I thought I could, but I can't. How could I have—how could we have—"

She was breathless; her panic terrified him. She was going to say the wrong thing, do the wrong thing, agree to anything Coakley asked and spend the rest of her life making up to him for having fallen in love with another man because, dammit, she *had* fallen in love with another man. That was why she'd gone to bed with him. Because she loved him. Only him.

And he loved her. Adored her! He'd been too dumb, too scared to admit it.

"Dana." He knew he sounded angry; he couldn't help it. It was fear that roughened his voice; he wanted to tell her that, but there wasn't time. "Keep quiet. Do you hear me? When they get here, let me do the talking. Don't—"

"Griffin," Cynthia said, "at last. We've been looking everywhere for you two!"

"Cynthia." His heart was pounding but his years of putting a good face on disaster in corporate boardrooms from New York to California came to his aid. He smiled easily, bent down and kissed her on the cheek.

"How did your meetings go?"

At least she'd stopped calling him "darling." Maybe that was a good sign. Hell, he thought desperately, he was willing to read tea leaves for a good sign.

"The meetings were fine," he said with false good humor. "Just fine."

"That's wonderful." Cynthia looked over her shoulder. "Isn't that wonderful, Arthur?"

Arthur nodded. "Wonderful," he said, but his eyes were darting from Griffin to Dana. Did he suspect something? He looked as if he did. Griffin spoke fast. He had to get Dana out of here and talk to her.

"Well," he said, "we'll see you late—"

"Dana?" Arthur's voice rolled right over his. This was definitely not a good sign, not from a man who'd been afraid to look him in the eye last night. "Dana, my dear, I want to talk to you."

"No," Griffin said. "You can't. Dana and I were just about to—we have an appointment, Coakley."

"Your appointment will have to wait. I have to talk to her now."

Dana clutched the table for support. Arthur knew. He knew! She didn't know how, but he knew. How else to explain his standing up to Griffin?

What a terrible thing she'd done! Arthur had flown all the way here to be with her, and what had she done in return? She'd slept with Griffin, even though she knew that Arthur was hoping that, someday, she'd fall in love with him. And the truth was, she never would, not in a million years, not even if—not even when—her affair with Griffin ended, and oh, what an ugly word that was, affair...

"Dana?" Arthur said.

Dana wrapped her arms around her middle. "Yes," she said

quietly, "all right. Let's go someplace quiet. I have to talk to you, too."

Everyone looked at her, Cynthia with polite curiosity, Arthur with concern, and Griffin with a look that said, don't be an idiot.

"I do," she whispered. "Really. I can't—I can't...I mean, I have to tell you—"

"Anderson."

Griffin's voice was blade-sharp. Dana turned toward him.

"I need to talk to Arthur," she said. "Alone."

"I'd advise against it."

"This doesn't concern you, Griffin."

"The hell it doesn't!" He leaned toward her, his eyes dark with rage. "Of course, it concerns me!"

Dana's mouth trembled. It was all so pitifully obvious. Griffin was afraid she'd tell Arthur what had happened, and Arthur would tell Cynthia, and then Griffin's chance to have his cake and eat it, too, would be lost.

Oh, Griffin, she thought, and her heart broke.

"You have nothing to worry about," she said. "This is between Arthur and me."

"Will you listen to me, dammit?"

"No." She cleared her throat, and worked hard to keep back the tears. "No, I won't. I know what I have to tell Arthur, and I'm going to do it."

Griffin's jaw tightened. "Then save it for New York, when you're not on the Data Bytes clock."

"Oh, my," Cynthia said nervously, "Griffin, really!"

"Keep out of this, please, Cynthia. Ms. Anderson is my employee. It's unfortunate that I have to remind her of that fact again, but if I must, I will."

"Listen here, McKenna, you can't talk to Dana that way. You have no right—"

"Who's going to stop me, Coakley? You?"

"Are you crazy?" Dana's voice rang out, loudly enough to stop conversation around them, but she was beyond caring.

"What's wrong with you, McKenna? Can't you tolerate it if people don't knuckle under at the sound of your voice?"

"Dana." Griffin tried to take her arm, but she shook him off. "Dana, take it easy. You don't know what you're saying. You're upset."

"You're damned right, I'm upset! I should never have let you talk me into taking this job, McKenna. Never!"

"Now, wait just a minute, Anderson. I didn't talk you into anything. *You* damn near blackmailed *me* into offering you a vice presidency."

"Hah!" Dana glared at him. "Maybe you've forgotten that you admitted to me, *boasted* to me, how you'd checked me out, gone through my résumé, set things up so I'd ask for a promotion you'd already decided to give me! But that's the way you are, isn't it? Always looking out for number one."

"Dana." Griffin spoke quietly, his eyes locked on hers, trying to turn things around before it was too late. "Dana, I'm asking you to listen to me."

"Say something worth hearing, then."

I love you, he thought... But there was Cynthia, looking bewildered, looking as if it would take little or nothing to make the tears start to flow, and he owed her better than this, dammit, better than telling her that he felt nothing for her in a room filled with strangers.

"You see, McKenna?" Dana's voice trembled. She had hoped, just for a moment... Oh, she had hoped... "You don't care, not for anybody but yourself. All right, then. I can see I've no choice but to tell you this, right now. I hadn't planned to. I'd intended to wait until we were back in New York, but..."

Griffin felt a coldness seeping through his bones. The Dana he'd held in his arms last night had vanished. The woman he saw in front of him now was stony-eyed with determination. She was the woman he'd known in New York.

"Go on, then," he said quietly. "Tell me now."

"Very well." She smiled, reached out to Arthur and curled

her hand around his arm. "Timothy Evans offered me a position with his company."

The room seemed to become very still. "And?"

"And..." She hesitated, then plunged ahead. "And, I intend to accept it." She smiled brightly, even though it was the hardest thing she'd ever done, even though she was about to compound one lie with another she'd have to live with for the rest of her life. "All I have to do now is convince Arthur that we'll both be happy, living in Boston." She saw the shock on Griffin's face, saw it give way to rage, and she smiled at Arthur, before she could do anything as stupid as weep. "We will, won't we?" she said.

And Arthur, poor dear, sweet Arthur, hesitated only briefly before saying yes.

CHAPTER TWELVE

How long did it take a sensible man to admit he'd come within a whisper of disaster?

A couple of hours, at the most.

Actually, not even that because Griffin had sorted it all out by the time he and Cynthia were on the six o'clock flight to New York.

What had happened between Dana Anderson and him had been—to put it down and dirty—good, hot sex. And that was no big surprise. The old horizontal tango was the inevitable result when you took a pair of healthy, attractive, unencumbered adults, dropped them into a tropical paradise, then stirred the mix by locking them into something euphemistically called the Bridal Suite.

But love? Griffin almost laughed. Love, as the song said, had nothing to do with it. Lust was the operative word here, and there was nothing wrong with that. He'd just let things get out of hand, that was all. His emotions. His behavior. And his treatment of Cynthia.

Poor Cynthia.

She sat beside him in the first-class compartment, eyes closed, hands folded demurely in her lap. His expression softened. Dear, gentle Cynthia. You'd never catch her putting on a display of temper, snarling and snapping like a cat with its back up. She hadn't once complained about the way he'd treated her, either.

Of course, she hadn't been in any position to complain. Flying down to join him had been her idea...

Griffin took a deep breath. Why try and blame this mess, or any part of it, on Cynthia? Okay, she'd delivered herself at his doorstep like a surprise package, but it had taken a lot of courage for her to do that. He should have let her know how much he admired that courage. And she shouldn't have been subjected to Dana's unladylike display of temper.

What a study in contrasts the two women were; Cyn with her eagerness to please, Dana with her tendency to bristle like a porcupine. Only a fool wouldn't have seen the difference, and known instantly which woman was one a man would want.

Cynthia was right for him. Of course, she was.

What an unholy mess he'd made of things. And for what reason? Why had he tried to put such a stupidly romantic spin on what had been nothing more than a weekend in the sack?

"Ridiculous," he muttered.

Cynthia looked at him. "Did you say something, Griffin?"

Her voice was gentle and ladylike, as always. He smiled, took her hand and patted it.

"It was nothing. Close your eyes, Cyn. Try and get some rest."

"Griffin. About this weekend..."

"I know," he said gently. "And I'm sorry. I promise, I'll make it up to you."

Cynthia gave a deep sigh. "Yes. I'm sure you will."

And he would.

It just amazed him that he'd been attracted to Dana at all. She was beautiful, yes, but so was Cynthia. Cynthia reveled in being feminine. Dana would probably sock a man in the eye if he so much as breathed the word in her direction.

Dana hadn't lied; he had to give her that much. She'd made it clear, right from the start, that she could play a man's game in a man's world. And she had. She'd gone after a better job right under his nose, as readily as she'd gone to bed with him. Oh, sure, she'd talked about feeling guilty but when you came right down to it, who wouldn't have felt guilty, considering the way they'd gone at each other even after Cynthia and the Bow Tie had turned up?

Sex. That's what it had been. But love? Love? No way. Dana hadn't fallen in love, and that was a damn good thing because neither had he.

Griffin's throat tightened.

Neither had he, he thought, and he turned his head and stared blindly out into the clouds.

Arthur and Dana couldn't book last-minute seats to Kennedy Airport, so they took a seven o'clock flight that would land them in Newark.

"We can take a taxi into Manhattan," Dana said, knowing that Arthur would probably tell her it was more efficient to take the bus, knowing, too, that she'd have to work at keeping her temper when he did because the last thing she gave a damn about just now was efficiency.

But he just nodded and said, yes, that would be fine.

As they buckled their seat belts, he turned and looked at her.

"Dana? Are you sure this is what you want to do?"

His face was ashen, but then, that was to be expected. She knew that she'd stunned him by accepting the proposal she'd spent so much time trying to avoid.

"I'm sure," she said, and gave him a quick smile.

Poor, dear man, she thought, and sighed. He must have been hoping she'd want to stay the rest of the weekend, to celebrate their engagement. Well, they would celebrate it. Certainly, they would...but not now. Not here, in the place where she'd behaved like just the sort of female she'd always despised, a round-heeled idiot who fell over backward the minute a man like Griffin McKenna gave her a smile.

What a self-centered, manipulative bastard he was! She'd gone into this knowing that he was a man who could have any woman, who thought women had been put on this earth for only one purpose—his pleasure—and what had she done? Played right into his hands, that was what! She'd let him talk her into sharing that damned suite, let him seduce her...

Dana's throat constricted. Who was she kidding? Griffin hadn't had to seduce her, she'd gone to him willingly, wantonly. She'd have stayed in his arms forever, if he'd wanted her.

No. No! She was romanticizing what had happened, rather than face the ugly truth, that she'd been sexually attracted to a man who might as well have been a stranger, a man whose beliefs were the opposite of her own...

"Dana?"

...*A man she'd wanted, with all her heart.*

"Dana. About this weekend..."

No, that was nonsense. Her heart had nothing to do with this. It was a different part of her anatomy that had ruled her behavior the past couple of days. She'd had a sleazy liaison with Griffin McKenna, and she'd treated Arthur—sweet, dear, kind, dependable Arthur—in a way he didn't deserve. But she'd make it up to him. She would. She'd spend the rest of her life, making it up to him.

"Dana," Arthur said again, and she turned to him, smiled, and took his hand.

"I know. It was an awful weekend, Arthur. But I promise, I'll make it up to you."

"No," he said quickly, "see, that's just the point. You don't need to—"

"I do," she said firmly, and managed a wobbly smile.

Arthur hesitated, as if he didn't quite believe her. Then he sighed.

"Yes," he said. "Yes, I'm sure you will."

He closed his eyes and, after a minute, Dana closed hers, too.

She *would* make it up to him. She'd marry him, become a good wife, learn to love him...

...*Learn not to think about Griffin.*

Tears seeped from under her lashes, and she turned her head away.

A month later, the special meeting Griffin had called at Data Bytes was drawing to a close—and not a minute too soon, as far as Jeannie Aarons was concerned.

Jeannie loved the elegance of computers, not the dullness of business reports, but that was what she'd been subjected to this morning, she and all the company's A-level employees. Slide shows from Sales. Pages of figures from Accounting. Brochures from Support. Jeannie had yawned and fought to stay awake through a litany of Projections, Predictions and Proposals...and what for?

The bottom line was simple enough.

Data Bytes was operating in the black.

Not that the information came as any great surprise. Things had turned around right after the Miami Beach conference. Griffin McKenna had brought back a stack of new clients, and Dana had brought back a big new job in Boston—and the announcement that she was engaged to marry Arthur.

Jeannie sighed. Married to Arthur. Dear, sweet, dull-as-dishwater Arthur.

A smattering of applause rolled through the boardroom, then grew stronger. McKenna was making his way to the microphone. Somebody whistled and McKenna grinned and held up his hands.

"You know," he said, "not very long ago, I had the feeling some of you people were figuring on throwing rotten tomatoes at me the next time we got together."

Everybody laughed.

"So, I'm doubly pleased that the news we've heard today is so good." He smiled. "And now I've got more good news. With the company on its feet again, I'm going to be pulling back from any hands-on management."

There were a couple of whistles, even an exaggerated, "No, not that!" McKenna laughed, along with the crowd.

"Yeah, well, I'm sure you'll get along just fine without me poking my nose where it doesn't belong—but before that happens, I want to tell you about your stock options."

The place erupted in cheers. Jeannie cheered, too. She'd have to tell Dana all about this when they had dinner together tonight. Not that stock options, or news about Data Bytes and McKenna would mean anything to Dana, considering her exciting new job in Boston, and the plans she was making for her future as Arthur's wife. Each time they spoke, Dana babbled on and on about how great things were—although, so far, there'd been no mention of a wedding date.

McKenna finished his announcement. People started to applaud.

"Champagne's on me," he said, and waved, but after shaking a few hands, Jeannie saw him slip out the door.

Ever since that Miami weekend, people said, he seemed to be all business.

She sighed. That Miami weekend. Sun-filled days, moon-kissed nights, in the company of a hunk like Griffin, and Dana had come back engaged to Arthur?

Heck. There was just no accounting for tastes.

Macy, the Dragon Lady, rang Jeannie at her desk and said McKenna wanted to see her.

Well, Jeannie thought, that was pleasantly unexpected. Maybe he'd finally noticed her. She fluffed up her hair, checked her makeup, and went down the hall to his office. Macy sent her straight in.

McKenna was standing with his back to his desk, looking out the window. Jeannie took a couple of seconds to admire the width of his shoulders before she spoke.

"Hi," she said brightly. "You sent for me?"

McKenna turned around. Jeannie frowned. She hadn't seen him close-up in weeks. Now that she did, she was kind of surprised. He was still as gorgeous as ever, but there were little lines around his eyes and a harsh set to his mouth that she didn't recall seeing before.

He had the general look of a man who needed a good night's sleep.

He motioned her to a chair, then wandered through a long explanation about wanting to be sure R and D was operating smoothly before he took off. Jeannie was even more surprised. He needed to query somebody on her level about as much as a dog needed to advertise for fleas.

Eventually, the peculiar conversation wound to a halt.

"Well," he said, and hesitated.

"Well?" Jeannie said, and waited.

McKenna shook his head. "Nothing. That's it, Ms. Aarons. That's, ah, that's all."

She nodded, and rose to leave. She was almost at the door when he called her name.

"Ms. Aarons?"

Jeannie turned and gave him her very best smile. "Jeannie," she said.

McKenna nodded. He was standing behind his chair and now he wrapped his hands around the back of it. She could see his knuckles whiten, and then he took a deep, deep breath.

"Jeannie. I was just wondering... I, ah, I mean..."

The phone on his desk buzzed. He frowned and punched a button. "What is it, Miss Macy? I thought I asked you to hold my calls."

"Yes, sir. But Miss Gooding is on the line. She wants to confirm your dinner appointment and tell you she may be a bit late."

"What dinner...?" Griffin sighed and ran his hand through his hair. "Of course. Tell her that's fine. Chez Maude at seven, and if she's late, I'll wait. Now, hold any other calls, please." He punched the button again, then looked at Jeannie. "What I'm trying to ask you, Ms. Aarons...Jeannie. What I'm trying to ask is—is..."

"Yes?" Jeannie said, trying not to let him see how puzzled she was. McKenna, stumbling for words? It didn't seem possible.

"I understand that you and Dana Anderson were good friends."

"Yes, sir. We still are."

"Do you hear from Ms. Anderson, then?"

"Oh, sure. We keep in touch. I'm meeting her for drinks this evening, as a matter of fact."

"She's in New York?"

Jeannie frowned. McKenna had said that the way she figured somebody might say, "You mean, there are life jackets on this boat?"

"Uh-huh. Dana's in on business. She and I are getting together, and then she's having dinner with her fiancé."

McKenna's mouth twisted. "Of course." He walked to the
window, stuffed his hands into his trouser pockets and stared
outside. "And what does she say? Is she happy?"

"Happy?" Jeannie relaxed. She understood now. Dana was
good at what she did, and McKenna was wondering if he could
hire her back. "Well, as far as I know, she likes her new job
well enough..."

"To hell with her job!" Griffin swung around. His eyes
were dark. "I'm asking you about Dana. About her life. Is she
happy?"

Wow, Jeannie thought. McKenna's face was like an open
book. It was there, right there, in his eyes, a need—a pain—
so raw and undisguised that it took her breath away. Whatever
had happened in Florida, it had to do with lots more than new
clients, job offers and Arthur's marriage proposal.

"Happy?" Jeannie echoed stupidly.

"Yes." Griffin glared at her. "Dammit, aren't I speaking
English? It's a simple question, Ms. Aarons. Please answer
it."

Jeannie considered. It wasn't such a simple question, now
that she thought about it. Dana said she was happy. In fact,
she said it all the time. Maybe she said it too often...and maybe
there was a darkness in Dana's eyes, too.

"I—don't know," Jeannie said. "That's the truth, Mr.
McKenna."

"Is she married yet?"

Jeannie hesitated. Then she tucked one hand into the pocket
of her skirt and crossed her fingers.

"Not yet," she said. "But the wedding's next month."

McKenna nodded. She waited for him to speak, but he
didn't. Instead, he walked back to the window and looked out.
The seconds rolled by. After a while, Jeannie tiptoed out of
the office and shut the door quietly after her.

She'd told McKenna a lie, a big one. And yet, somehow, it

had felt more as if what she'd told him was that yes, there *were* life jackets on this boat, and tossed one to him.

Right or wrong, whatever happened now, it was out of her hands.

Dana hurried along Third Avenue toward the place where she'd agreed to meet Jeannie, and wished she'd canceled the appointment.

It wasn't that she didn't want to see Jeannie. She did. It was just that there was so much to do back in Boston. Her new job, her new apartment, her plans for the future...

How could she deal with all that, if she was in New York?

Besides, New York wasn't part of her life anymore. Her job, her old apartment...it was all in the past.

And so was Griffin.

Dana's pace quickened. As ridiculous as it was, he'd been on her mind all day. And that *was* ridiculous, because she never thought about him anymore. Why would she? Her memories of him, of that weekend, were an embarrassment. Not just what she'd done with Griffin, but what she'd told herself she felt for him.

Love. Love? What a joke. She'd given in to some very basic sexual urges, and then she'd lied to herself about it. *That* was the real humiliation, that she, of all people, should have found it necessary to justify her behavior by trying to bathe it in the pink glow of romance.

All right, so she did still think about him. Not often, though, just every now and then, when she saw a man with a walk like Griffin's, or heard a laugh like his. And there were times she dreamed about him, too.

Silly, when sex was all it had been, all it could ever have been.

Except, it wasn't sex she dreamed about. She dreamed about lying safe in his arms. About doing all the things they'd never had time to do—walking along the beach or going for a drive in the country. Talking, strolling hand in hand, sharing their lives and their hopes...

"Hey, lady, watch where you're goin'."

Dana murmured an excuse as somebody maneuvered past her. Great. Just great. Here she was, so caught up in her own pointless thoughts that she was bumping into strangers on the street. Why hadn't she flown back to Boston? That had been her intention when she'd phoned Jeannie to cancel their appointment late this afternoon, but Jeannie hadn't given her the chance.

"No time to chat," Jeannie had said briskly. "We can talk later, at this great new place. Chez Maude. Meet me there at seven, okay?"

Dana sighed. Another pretentious restaurant. Flowers. Candles. A menu that was impossible to decipher. And there it was now, just ahead. She'd told Arthur to meet her here, too. Sevenish, she'd said, because she wanted to give Jeannie a chance to get to know him and like him. Arthur was a good person. And perceptive. He seemed to understand that she needed time to get used to the idea of marrying him. He hadn't pressured her at all. He hadn't even mentioned marriage since that night they'd flown back from Florida.

Arthur had his good points. Really, he did.

It's just that he wasn't Griffin.

The tears, and the despair, came without warning. Dana started to cry just as she reached the restaurant door. She couldn't see Jeannie tonight, nor Arthur. And she knew, with stunning certainty, that she *couldn't* marry Arthur, not like this, not ever. She started to step back, but it was too late. The door to the restaurant opened, a man stepped out, they collided...

...And Dana stumbled straight into Griffin's arms.

Griffin had been standing in Chez Maude's tiny entryway, as uncomfortable as a prisoner waiting for the jury's verdict, telling himself that no matter how bad it was, he'd manage to tough it out.

It seemed dead wrong to be meeting Cynthia for dinner when his mind was filled with Dana, and that made him angry as hell.

Why should he be thinking about Dana? There wasn't a reason in the world. And what an ass he'd made of himself today with Jeannie Aarons. Asking those silly questions about a woman he was never going to see again. Never wanted to see again. He had to put Dana aside and get on with his life, and the way to do that, he knew, was to leave the past behind him.

It was time to make a commitment to Cynthia.

She was right for him. She'd fit into his life without causing a ripple. She was easy to get along with, gentle, kind, amenable to his every wish. She'd never give him a hard time or argue with his decisions.

And he'd never love her.

Well, so what? A good marriage should be structured like a good corporation. It needed a solid base, and he would surely have that with Cynthia. Their lives would be comfortable, pleasant...and dull.

Life with Dana would never have been dull. It would have been filled with the spark of disagreement and the joy of reconciliation, with a passion so intense it could make his heart sing just to remember what it had been like to hold her in his arms.

"Bloody hell," he muttered, and he swung around and pulled open the restaurant door.

He didn't want a comfortable life, he wanted a joyful one.

He wanted Dana.

She was out there, somewhere. And he wasn't going to rest until he found her and made her admit that she loved him and not the Bow Tie, even if he had to force the admission from her with his kisses, if he had to find out where she was going to be married and abduct her from the altar.

"Yes," he said as he stepped onto the sidewalk—and Dana stumbled into his arms.

They stared at each other in stunned silence.

"Griffin?"

"Dana?"

Oh, she thought, how she had missed him! Her legs were

weak, just at the sight of him. If only—if only, by some miracle...

Yes, he thought, oh, yes. This was the other half of his own soul. His heart was already hammering against his ribs. She had to love him, dammit, she had to.

"I..." She made a little fluttering motion with her hands. "I didn't expect—"

"No," He cleared his throat. "Neither did—"

"Griffin," she said breathlessly, "Griffin, I—I—"

Tell him. Tell him the truth, Dana, that you love him with all your heart. Because you do. You know you do. You know you'll always love him...

"Dana." Griffin stared at the face he'd dreamed of, at the woman who held his life in her hands. "Dana," he said... *Hell, man! Don't be an idiot.* "You can't marry Arthur," he said, rushing the words together. "I won't let you."

"You won't...?" Dana stared at him. "Really, McKenna, you can't just..."

"I can," he said, "and I will. Dammit, Anderson, you are not going to marry that man!"

"Of course I can. I mean, I could. I mean..."

"You can't." Griffin's eyes narrowed. "You're going to marry me, instead."

"What?" Dana whispered. "What?"

Griffin took a deep breath. "I said...oh, hell, Anderson! Come here."

He reached out and took hold of her. For one long, endless moment, she held back. Then, just when he feared he had lost her forever, a smile began to tremble on her lips.

"Oh, Griffin," she whispered, and then she was in his arms.

He kissed her and kissed her, and she kissed him back. His arms tightened around her, until she could hardly breathe; her arms rose and she twined them around his neck.

"Dana," he said against her mouth, "my darling Dana."

"Griffin, I missed you so much—"

He kissed her again, his hands clasping her face. "I love you," he whispered. "With all my heart."

Dana sighed. "Tell me again."

He did, with another kiss that left her swaying against him.

"When you said you were going to marry Coakley," he murmured, "I almost went crazy."

"Me, too. When I realized you were trying to protect Cynthia—"

"Protect Cynthia?"

"Uh-huh." Dana touched the tip of her tongue to her lips. "You know, keep her from knowing about us, because you loved her."

"Oh, sweetheart. We've got some talking to do. Cyn's a nice girl, but I never loved her."

"And I never loved Arthur."

"Didn't you?"

Dana shook her head. "You're the only man I've ever loved, Griffin McKenna."

"Damn right," he said gruffly, while his heart swelled with joy. "Not just the only, but the first and the last. Any arguments about that?"

"Not a one," she said softly.

Griffin's arms tightened around her. "When I think of all the time we wasted..."

Dana went up on her toes and put her mouth to his, kissing him with a tenderness and a passion that he'd known only in her arms.

"I thought I'd lost you," he whispered.

"I know. I thought what we'd had—what we'd found...that those memories would be all I had to live on for the rest of my life."

Griffin drew back, just far enough so he could see Dana's face. Her eyes glowed with joy and with tears. He kissed them away and thought how close he'd come to losing her. The realization made his own eyes feel suspiciously damp.

"Anderson," he said gruffly.

She smiled and touched a fingertip to his mouth. "Yes, McKenna?"

He lowered his head and leaned his forehead against hers.

"I am not an easy man to live with," he said.

Her smile tilted. "Do tell."

"I'm opinionated. And maybe just a little bit egotistical."

"A little bit," she said agreeably.

"I tend to be very protective of what is mine."

"That's quite a speech, McKenna. Are you telling me, perhaps, that there's a hint of male chauvinism in you?"

"Me?" A grin spread across his handsome face. "Well, it's possible." Their eyes met, and his smile faded. "Anderson?"

"Yes?"

"When are we going to get married?"

"When? *When?* There you go, McKenna. You haven't even asked me if I *want* to marry you. Here you are, taking charge, barking out orders, assuming..."

"Shut up, Anderson," Griffin said, and kissed her. After a while, Dana sighed and leaned back in his encircling arms.

"Next week," she said dreamily. "Is that too soon?"

"Well, I didn't want to rush you..." He smiled. "How about this weekend?"

"This weekend sounds wonder... Oh, Griffin." Dana's face fell. "Griffin, we forgot."

"What, sweetheart?"

"How are we going to break the news to Arthur and Cynthia?"

"Hell." Griffin sighed and rested his hands on Dana's shoulders. "It's going to be rough."

"Arthur will be devastated."

"Yeah, so will Cynthia."

"I know." Dana frowned and gazed past Griffin's shoulder. "Well, we'll just have to do what has to be—what has to be..." Her breath caught. "Arthur?"

"Where?" Griffin looked around. "Be brave, sweetheart. Let me handle..." Griffin jerked back as his bewildered gaze fell on a couple locked in embrace a few feet away. "Cyn?"

Cynthia and Arthur turned toward Griffin and Dana.

"Hello, Griffin," Cynthia said shyly. "We—we just...

Arthur and I happened to come along at the same time. And we saw you two—I mean, we couldn't help but overhear..."

"Cynthia and I fell in love that weekend in Miami Beach," Arthur said. He stood tall, his arm locked around Cynthia's waist. He blushed. "Love at first sight, you know? We've been waiting and waiting to tell you, but—"

"But there just never seemed to be the right moment to do it," Cynthia said. "And we didn't want to hurt you."

"We finally decided we'd each break the news tonight." Arthur cleared his throat. "We were concerned how you'd react, but—"

"But," Cynthia said, leaning her head against his shoulder, "it looks to us as if everything's worked out just fine."

Dana smiled as she turned to Griffin. "I think that's an understatement."

"Oh," Griffin said lazily, "I don't know, Anderson. For instance, I've changed my mind about getting married this weekend." He lifted her face to his. "What would you say to tomorrow?"

Dana laughed, but her eyes filled with tears of happiness. "I'd say it's the best idea you've ever had, McKenna," she said.

Griffin didn't argue. He knew she was right.

The merger of Anderson and McKenna paid its first dividend three years later.

It was a boy, a healthy, beautiful son, weighing seven pounds, six ounces. He had his father's blue eyes, his mother's golden hair, and when he was old enough to leave for a long weekend with his proud grandmother, his parents celebrated the occasion with a joyous return visit to the Bridal Suite at the Hotel de las Palmas on the sands in Miami Beach.

Take 2 bestselling love stories FREE

Plus get a FREE surprise gift!

Special Limited-Time Offer

Mail to Harlequin Reader Service®

3010 Walden Avenue
P.O. Box 1867
Buffalo, N.Y. 14240-1867

YES! Please send me 2 free Harlequin Presents® novels and my free surprise gift. Then send me 6 brand-new novels every month, which I will receive months before they appear in bookstores. Bill me at the low price of $3.12 each plus 25¢ delivery and applicable sales tax, if any*. That's the complete price, and a saving of over 10% off the cover prices—quite a bargain! I understand that accepting the books and gift places me under no obligation ever to buy any books. I can always return a shipment and cancel at any time. Even if I never buy another book from Harlequin, the 2 free books and the surprise gift are mine to keep forever.

106 HEN CH69

Name	(PLEASE PRINT)	
Address		Apt. No.
City	State	Zip

This offer is limited to one order per household and not valid to present Harlequin Presents® subscribers. *Terms and prices are subject to change without notice. Sales tax applicable in N.Y.

UPRES-98   ©1990 Harlequin Enterprises Limited

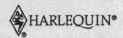

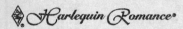

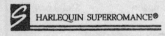

Don't miss these Harlequin favorites by some of our bestselling authors!

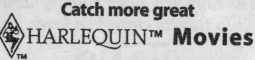

The only way to be a bodyguard
is to stay as close as a lover...

STAND
BY ME

The relationship between bodyguard and client is always
close...sometimes too close for comfort. This September,
join in the adventure as three bodyguards, protecting three
very distracting and desirable charges, struggle not to cross
the line between business and pleasure.

STRONG ARMS OF THE LAW
by Dallas SCHULZE

NOT WITHOUT LOVE
by Roberta LEIGH

SOMETIMES A LADY
by Linda Randall WISDOM

Sometimes danger makes
a strange bedfellow!

Available September 1998 wherever
Harlequin and Silhouette books are sold.

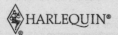 

Look us up on-line at: http://www.romance.net

PHBR998

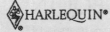 

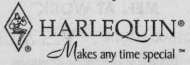